THE FRIED–EGG QUILT

THE FRIED–EGG QUILT

A Pioneer Journey to Arizona Territory

with illustrations by Diane Yi

Laura Ostrom

iUniverse, Inc.

New York Lincoln Shanghai

The Fried–Egg Quilt
A Pioneer Journey to Arizona Territory

iUniverse, Inc.

For information address:
iUniverse, Inc.
2021 Pine Lake Road, Suite 100
Lincoln, NE 68512
www.iuniverse.com

ISBN: 0-595-32745-1

Contents

Foreword

The major human story of the 19th century was the movement of people from the Old World to the New World, and their westward flow across the new land. *The Fried-Egg Quilt*, presented in the form of Molly McGinnis' Journal is a microcosm of that flow. It portrays the experiences and emotions of the mother of a small family migrating from Lima, Ohio to Arizona Territory in 1865, and settling in the pioneer village later named Prescott.

The author, Laura Ostrom writes from a background of 40 years of teaching, tutoring, and raising children, over 90 years of living in the East, the Midwest and the West, and a lifetime interest in the history of America and its people.

Carl E. Ostrom

Introduction

In a week we shall be on our way to Arizona Territory. We've been gathering and organizing supplies for over two months, still I can scarcely contemplate such a journey and perhaps I should not go. How well I remember tales told by Mother and Father when they traveled from Rhode Island to settle here in Ohio. It was a wearisome and dangerous undertaking, full of privations. Theirs were frightening memories. But today is different. We are not repeating history. Development has brought changes. These are modern times. Wagons are sturdier, more commodious. Today there are well known trails that have been found agreeable by the folks who have traveled them. There are settlements established where there were none when I was born. The travel of today is far safer than thirty years ago. We should not be concerned that it is so dangerous a journey.

Of course it will not be short, and it will not be as casual as home life—certainly not. Modern conveniences make one lazy. Here I have a pump installed in the kitchen. Out there, wherever that will be, I may be fortunate to have a spring nearby, or a stream that I can walk to. I know we will do without kerosene lights as coal oil is too dear and burdensome to transport across the country. My beautiful lamps remain here. I will not fret about that for these lamps will bring pleasure to those left behind. There! That phrase I must learn to avoid. "Our dear ones left behind" sounds a bell of dread within me. My, how I seem to vacillate! First, determined and eager to fly away, then fettered with anguish and reluctant to move. But I do have it clear in my mind. I will go. I will follow my restless husband wherever he may go. None shall ever say I hesitated. It is my duty and my happiness to be with my mate. I shall not be looking back.

Father, at last consenting that I go, is a treasure lode for planning. Today he suggested I think of the things I use most then think of ways to do without them. "That will prepare you for four months in a covered wagon," he said.

Food and water, of course, we must have. As I look into the Conestoga wagon today I think I need not worry about what I shall take of my own things. There is scant room remaining. Such quantities of food! One hundred fifty pounds of bacon, barrels of corn, beans, rice, sugar, and even tins of coffee and tea. Such huge provisions make it difficult to feel concerned that there might ever be days when food will be gone, that we may be sorely tried to find sustenance to keep body and soul together. It has happened to some travelers in the past. We are well prepared. Mac is a planner of great foresight. He will know what best to take and leave. In God and Mac I fully entrust my life, and hope it is not sacrilegious to state it so.

The water kegs will hang on the outside, Mac explained. Even so there is now only a narrow path in the middle of the wagon bed. The tent and blankets will go there and make a daytime resting place. I cannot imagine resting in the middle of the day. Of my own personal needs and supplies I shall be frugal. My trunk will be half filled with my clothing, one extra dress and three petticoats. Mac's and little Virgil's extra clothes will fill the trunk along with the medicines packed for safety and convenience. I have planned carefully that the oil of camphor not be spilled! My rolls of yarn for knitting as we travel will not be packed but suspended in a waterproof pouch from the canvas wagon cover. As I mentally prepare myself for a closely packed life I find even my letter formations becoming increasingly diminished. I am truly constricting my life!

CHAPTER 1

The Fried-Egg Quilt

Monday: My excitement increases as we plan for and obtain all the supplies for our long journey to Arizona Territory. It is a sturdy task. Various piles grow then gradually disappear down into their labeled barrel. Dear husband, Mac, has everything well planned. Of course his own farm tools, blacksmithy equipment, and general supplies, he has planned for first. The time will come when he needs to repair something. While we are on the trail the barn will not be handy by to pick up some needed piece of metal or an extra board. Indeed he has a difficult task.

My kind of planning is a bit different. All dry food supplies must last several weeks and then be replenished as needed in the town we will be passing through. A barrel each of bacon, flour, sugar, salt, meal, and a large box of tea are quantities I can scarcely believe necessary, though it is a certainty that we will run out of some supplies before we want to. I pray that it is never water. We plan always to keep a two-barrel supply. Some possibilities are a bit disquieting to allow to enter one's thoughts.

Suddenly, now my mind is overwhelmed with the unexpected departure of Mother and Father tomorrow. I scarce can contain my composure. This day will be finished helping my dear parents prepare for their travel. Father has just now received word to come to Brown's Crossing, 20 miles east of here, to minister to a young family whose aged parents have both passed to their heavenly reward. How sad to lose both parents at one time.

I do grieve for my selfish self, though. How I wanted my Mother's loving arms about me one more time as we depart for Arizona Territory two days hence. We never outgrow the need and love of our parents. I was overcome when Father told me of the changed plans. Tenderly, he quietly brushed a tear from my cheek, then exploded into a joyous romp with little Virgil to break the tension of the moment. I must go tend to the bread-baking for Mother while she packs supplies and clothing. Tomorrow I can finish the packing of our little family's bedding and clothing. I go with a heavy heart to my duties.

Tuesday: Father and Mother have driven away from us. With a sinking, hollow feeling beyond description we have reversed our farewells. Their eager team, prancing in the cold morning air, was the only sign of happiness as we waved our last good-byes. I pray we will greet again before we meet in the heavenly shore.

When Virgil and I could no longer hear the disappearing horse hoofs we returned to the house and began to fill the big wood-box behind the cookstove. It was best we busy ourselves at something more strenuous than tears. I am too sad to write more at present. I will read to Virgil.

Tuesday eve: I must be especially mindful of where I secure Mother's parting gift to me—her locket. In it are newly made pictures of her and Father—a precious treasure that I must guard always, perhaps in my white stockings.

Wednesday: The almanac and the red sunset of last evening have foretold the weather will be cold and clear for the remainder of the week. The wagons are loaded with all our provisions for man, beast, and hammer. Be still my pounding heart. Today I must finish the packing of bedding and clothing

The clothing problem is simple. We will take the three outfits we each have. As we ride along I will be mending as needed, even stitching up new items as we need them. I have three pieces of yard goods and several sugar sacks that will be all we need before we cross the wide Missouri. I must think of a careful, handy, yet safe place to keep my sewing basket. Needles are very hard for store keepers to keep in supply since the terrible war in the states.

Bedding will take up more space than our clothing. I plan for two covers over each person and one folded under each person. That should be comfortable sleeping. Mattress ticking will be best for sheets and pillow cases, and of course three pillows will be needed.

Mac will never notice what covers he is using but Virgil will never be parted from his fried-egg quilt. Worn, torn, mended and patched, we cannot allow it to wear out. His grandmother made it before Virgil was a year old. It was one of his first words. "Egg," he said, pointing to the daisy pattern's yellow center. It was the fried-egg quilt from then on and always his favorite cover. It may not last the whole journey. I think Virgil would even learn to sew to keep his fried-egg quilt from wearing out. Yes, it must travel with us and be mended as need be.

Wednesday eve: Tomorrow, tomorrow, March second, 1865, we leave for Arizona Territory! My dear husband, Mac, in his stalwart assurance, knows all is in readiness. He is ready to crack the whip over the team's ears. Our second wagon, loaded with animal food and tools, will be driven by our friend, Little Cloud, of the Hopewell Indian Tribe.

He, too, knows the elderly Frenchman, Mr. Truffat, who has made this western trip three times as a guide. He has been invaluable to Mac in making decisions for general planning of what to take and how much. A barrel of bacon does seem a great deal but there are very few smoke houses along the way. It is chancy to plan on bear meat and bear fat. For certain, bacon won't go to waste.

CHAPTER 2

First Day Out

Thursday, March 2, 1865

Today the whips snapped, the four teams strained and the wagon wheels broke from the frozen mud. We were bundled in the two well-packed Conestoga wagons, ready and off for Arizona Territory!

Virgil's blonde head was covered over his ears with the red woolen cap his grandmother knitted, his coat buttoned snugly to the chin, a scarf over all. I, too, was warmly dressed but I thought surely my joy was shining through the blankets that covered us.

The warm bodies of the two double teams steamed in the frosty morning air. Their breathing flowed dragon smoke ahead of them, according to Virgil. His lively 5-year-old imagination was active and happy.

"I see a finger of light peeking under the black, ragged cloud," he smiled at me. "The sun is going to be surprised to find us gone," he shivered in pleasure.

Mac's red, frost-tinged beard hid his somber face. His is a serious job. He nodded to Little Cloud, our Indian friend, the second driver, standing straight and regal beside his wagon and two mule teams. Little Cloud returned Mac's signal, pulled forward, then to one side so Mac could pass through the gateway to become the lead wagon. Little Cloud closed the squeaking iron gate behind us forever.

I hid my face in my woolen scarf lest I give a sign of my thrill of excitement. I would not want to look or sound like a silly schoolgirl. I did not attempt to glance back. I did not need to. I lived there all my twenty-five years and will always hold dear in my memory that little white home beneath the great elms.

As we moved down the street, neighbors came out to wave us on in the semi-darkness. Their bright doorways shed a surprised, cheerful note to our leave-taking of Lima, Ohio. It was so unexpected that a mixture of sadness and happiness gripped me, but I waved and smiled through it all. Mac is a wonderful husband. I am mighty proud of his readying us for this great journey that will end in Arizona Territory, a "Strange Somewhere" far away.

Now I am relieved that Mother and Father had to leave yesterday. Father had burial rites to give for a parishioner in Brown's Crossing 20 miles east of us. To leave my home, my hometown, to part from my parents all in the same instant would have brought on an unseemly flow of emotions. Father, again, might have thought to urge us to remain. I am happy that the discussion was ended long ago.

Rule Number One has been established. No one will jump from the moving wagon. When the horses have stopped each of us may climb down properly. It is a rule for Virgil, of course, least he jump and be run over, or jump and injure an ankle when landing on rough ground. Taking care is better than having regrets.

Another understanding is that there will be a five-minute rest every hour for man and beast, including me. Being the only woman, at present, there are no wide skirts to shelter me when I need to pause for private duties. Using the chamber pot in the wagon is the most awkward part of my day. Now having managed that, I know I can. Dear Mac disposed of it for me. Land sakes, such consideration.

Before he left for Brown's Crossing, Father presented his beautiful gold watch to Mac. What a kind and loving thing to do. I did not know of it until Mac consulted the watch for the time of day. He is mighty proud of that watch but keeps it fastened out of sight. It will also be useful as a compass when we need one. He will show us later.

Today Virgil and I walked to get warm or rode if we needed to rest. The hazy sunlight shone mildly warm but not directly in our eyes. We are traveling northwest; the sun is in the southeast.

Mac walked alongside the wagon at times. Little Cloud walked all the time, as is his custom. He is a fine person. Mac respects him highly for his knowledge of the road as well as his competence in any emergency. Already I feel the loss that will be ours when he leaves us in Missouri.

Mac is pleased with both the mule and horse teams. They have pulled the heavily loaded wagons well. The loads are well packed and no time has been lost in repacking loose ends.

Without tiring our teams unduly, we are traveling about two miles an hour. Our twelve mile trip will take about six hours. Soon after the nooning we should be at the home of Elijah Clark, Mac's friend of Gettysburg war days. We will have time to make ourselves look presentable. I am surely looking forward to meeting the Clarks and their young relatives, the Bunselmeier family.

New Friends

The Clarks and Bunselmeiers

On our arrival at the Elijah Clarks' comfortable clapboard home, Mac sent Virgil on a manly task. "You best go check on the keg of horseshoe nails in Little Cloud's wagon, son. We don't want them spilling about."

The boy trotted off importantly and met young Matthew, the ten-year-old son of the Clarks, and the Clarks' son-in-law, Winfield Bunselmeier.

Winfield and Mac were hospitalized in Gettysburg during part of this cruel War Between the States. They vowed that if they lived through the experience they would make this great journey westward. Virgil learned most of this information before I lighted from the wagon.

I could see right off that our new friends would be comfortable people to know and travel with. As bid by Mr. Clark, I entered the pleasant home, hung my heavy wraps on the door hook and stepped to the fireplace to warm myself. Not until then did I realize I was a bit cold. No one was present so I lifted my skirts a trifle, thrust my feet forward and warmed them until my shoe buttons were hot. How enjoyable.

Just then Mrs. Clark, or Catherine, as she asked me to call her, came slowly in guiding a tiny old crone, her grandmother, to a chair at the fire. Grandma Clark nodded pleasantly in my direction, took up her knitting, the needles soon clicking away.

Catherine explained that Granny could see only poorly, heard nothing and rarely spoke, but enjoyed the world about her. She would not be going on the long trek to Missouri, of course. Catherine's sister, with family of four, would be living with Granny on our departure. A very pleasant arrangement.

A young lady entered the room and I met Catherine's daughter, Blanche, a sweet girl, charming as her mother. Blanche and Winfield had been newlyweds since November. This is to be a great adventure for all of us! Gone are all unspoken thoughts of traveling with strangers.

We heard the men's feet stomping the back porch. They had given the horses and mules their rub-down, food, water, and pulled down their hay for the night. Having washed up outside the kitchen door, the men were ready to put their feet under the table and partake heartily of a bountiful supper.

They sat comfortably with their backs to the range enjoying the heat. Blanche and Catherine waited on the men, of course. No help would they have from me, though I am not accustomed to sit and eat with the menfolks. When the pies had been cut and passed, the two women came to join us.

After supper the conversation picked up with no lag. We spoke of our day's journey, the preparations the Clarks had made, the events before us. With the drone of voices Virgil fell asleep at the supper table. Blanch carrying a lantern, took me up to the loft. Cornhusk ticks under plump feather tick with quilts over all, made a most inviting sleeping spot for our family.

When the table was redd up, the dishes washed, dried and set out on the table for breakfast, we all took to our beds as soon as possible. Both Mac and Elijah Clark insisted that Little Cloud sleep indoors, not in the woodshed. He chose the kitchen floor. Tomorrow would be another early leave-taking; we all have need of a sound night's sleep. Most likely there will be an early leave-taking for the next six months.

As I climbed to the loft I thought how pleasant the trip will be neighboring with Catherine on the way to Missouri.

CHAPTER 4

Eight Bits for Leather

On our second day out we have again had good traveling. In only seven hours we arrived in Van Wert, a distance of fifteen miles. Virgil and Matthew each rode in his own family's wagon but the minute we stopped they were a happy pair. Of course they come obediently when called. They will be good company for each other.

Van Wert, the county seat of Van Wert County, is a sizeable town of seven hundred. I have never been here before. In fact I have never been so far from home before.

The men and the two boys took their leave of us women to go horse trading. Blanche knew her way about town and took us to the leather market. I felt very daring traveling about without my husband.

The leather market was astonishing. Blanche found her way among the great stacks of deer hides that were piled in heaps like so many huge stacks of ragged pancakes. Some were rolled yet in tattered bundles. The hunters and trappers bring in these dried, green hides each spring after their winter's toil. Teamsters take heaped wagon loads of hides to the tannery.

These green hides did not interest Blanche. We needed soft, tanned hides for our use. The best price we found was three hides for two bits. I had to consider a minute whether Mac would think I was squandering 25 cents unnecessarily and decided he would not mind. I bought six black and six brown hides and felt involved in a great business deal.

Two young boys were dispatched to carry all our purchases to Mac's wagon. They had no more than returned when we women found a great bargain—ready-made leather trousers and coats at little more than the price we had just paid. I went in search of Mac at the livery stable just down the street. I would need more money. I had started shopping with a dollar and two bits, thinking that would be a plenty. Living high on the hog costs money.

I found Mac and politely made my request when I noticed he had a great cud of tobacco in his jaw. Seeing outrage on my face he quietly turned, spat in the straw, returned with a placid smile and handed me a five dollar bill. I am still laughing to myself about it. I had never intended to ask for so large a sum, but I surely would have made an angry remark at his squandering money on chewing tobacco. It was the closest I have ever come to having a spat in public with Mac and he settled it with his good humor and generosity.

I bought coats for us three at a dollar-a-piece and had enough to buy trousers for Virgil and me. Mac has a pair. Leather clothes may not be very fashionable, but as Catherine pointed out, we will travel warmly.

In addition, at the last minute, I wickedly bought a beautiful grey-fox muff with my last two bits.

CHAPTER 5

Angus (Mac) McGinnis

I write this for Virgil. When he is a grown man he will want to know what life was like for his Paw as a boy. He will want to know how his Paw stood in the War Between the States. He should really know his Paw for he is a fine man.

Mac has a pleasant easy laugh. While yet a young boy he learned the importance of finding joy in his life to balance against an uphill, rocky climb. When Mac's mother died his father never faltered in his responsibility to his seven-year-old son. As was often done, he did not farm Mac out as someone's unpaid help. He taught his son that grief and mourning are a part of life, intermingled with the comforts and joys of life's daily toil.

Fortunately, Mac had neighbors who offered him plenty of toil. He was the only boy handy by to hire for chores. He kept woodboxes full and cleaned chicken houses.

Dumping the chicken refuse on the kitchen gardens, Mac delighted in watching the snowstorm of feathers blow in the spring wind. Cleaning stables was harder work but that was no reason for avoiding it. He learned that even a gentle buggy horse could give a sharp kick. His face bore a shoe mark on his nose and chin to show for it.

One of the elderly neighbors provided Mac with a special joy. He taught him to read. Schooling did not begin for Mac until he was nine. The bigger boys soon learned that the gangling first-grade boy was not to be the butt of their jokes and pranks. His strength, as well as reading, put him well above them, but he was a friend to all. Ciphering had begun early, too, when his father taught him to keep records of his time and money at two bits a month.

This quiet, energetic boy at age twelve was apprenticed to a blacksmith and wheelwright. Because it was necessary to wear boots and gloves in the shop, Mac learned the trade of tanning leather and leather working in his spare time. He was no longer a barefooted laborer. Eventually, the best buggies in town were upholstered by Mac's handiwork.

Mac's mind developed along with his understanding and enjoyment of people. He knew few men who mistreated their horses or dogs. Of those who did, he saw that they in turn had been mistreated in their youth. The ill fortune of circumstances taught Mac compassion for his fellowmen, reinforced by the gentle teachings of his father.

A slave auctioneer, traveling through Mac's home town of Medina, Ohio, had observed Mac shoeing horses, liked what he saw, and demanded speedy service. Mac acknowledged the man's need, yet assured him that only quality work would come from this shop. The auctioneer looked sharply at the smithy's muscular 6-foot-3-inches. He did not miss the blue eyes with no frown of annoyance. He saw a penetrating gaze that showed a direct connection between words and intentions.

Thinking to ease any strain in their relationship the stranger eventually asked Mac if he would be interested in the idea of being a helper at slave auctions. Traveling about the countryside would be entertaining, the man suggested.

Mac raised his red-brown head from his work, his towering figure standing straight. His tanned face flushed brightly as though he held his breath. When the suppressed anger subsided, Mac thundered his answer, "No!" without giving the customer the courtesy of a glance.

It was at about this time in his life that Mac came to Lima, Ohio to set up his own farrier business. I met Angus McGinnis, at a church meeting. We were wed the next year. You, Virgil, were born two years later.

Joining the Northern Forces in the cruel War Between the States, Mac wanted to give his support to Lincoln's efforts to make freemen of the slaves. No one should be held in bondage. Furthermore, all should be given the chance to learn to read and become educated. Our Virginia statesman, Thomas Jefferson, had said it must be so.

And so it was that your Paw fought bravely in The Cause for Freedom. A rifle ball in his left thigh put him in the hospital. There he nearly lost his life from the infection that followed. It happened to many brave men. Mac's wound finally healed; his fever subsided. As soon as he was strong enough to get about he offered his services in his ward of 50 men. Nurses were scarce and sorely overworked.

At that time, your Paw met his friend, Winfield Bunselmeier; likewise a recovered soldier, giving a hand in the hospital. Winfield's home was on the western edge of the developed states.

Missouri was a free state. No slaves were allowed to be bought or sold nor brought into the state even if they had long been owned by their master. Free state it was, but sorely divided in opinion. Winfield wanted to rejoin his family in Missouri and help the cause of freemen to flourish.

Mac's plan was to live and work in Arizona Territory to prevent slavery from developing as it had in some parts of the southwest. So it was that our two families joined in their western trek, traveling together as far as Missouri.

Yes, Virgil, you can be mighty proud of your father, Angus McGinnis. A fine person, is Mac. You are growing to be very like him, my son.

CHAPTER 6

Hurry On

We have been on our journey for five days. All goes well. Each night we have been able to stay with friends or acquaintances of friends. The arrangements have been most pleasant. They have even insisted on our taking a packed lunch for our noon-day meal. Such kind hospitality speeds us on our way before sunrise.

We have traveled nearly 15 miles a day. Mac says today we will cross the state line into Indiana. I realize it is not important but I have never before been out of my home state, Ohio.

I am aware of the worriment, a mental concern within myself. I feel I surely have the thoughts of those early sailors 400 years ago. No familiar landmark was in sight. It gave them a searing spot of fear that grew in the mind, daily wondering had they gone too far? Would they be able to find their way home? And, importantly, why had they ever consented to leave home port?

Then I shake myself. This is 1865. Of course all those are not truly my own thoughts or fears but without Mac's stalwart guidance and knowledge they might well be mine too.

Even so, I have a strange feeling. I am suspended in time and space. I do not know where I am so I am nowhere. From here I am going to an unknown, strange place. But I go willingly and always I will be with my family. I shall put aside shallow fears.

It has been a blessing to have this fine traveling weather. At dawn Virgil is busy blowing his breath in long white clouds into the freezing cold air, never minding the temperature. He says he is thawing out and makes no complaint.

For that I am grateful for we have such an urge to hurry on and cross the streams while they are still frozen.

CHAPTER 7

Fishing at Ft. Wayne, Indiana

Yesterday we traveled 20 miles to Hicksville, Indiana. I was so weary I could not write. Today we traveled 18 miles to Ft. Wayne, Indiana. We have had beautiful sunny weather though cold at night. Good weather for running maple sap. We have seen only two maple groves being worked.

The men in our group had need to visit the farrier and wheelwright there in Ft. Wayne. Blanche and her mother are with the Chinese laundryman with Matthew as their helper.

Virgil and I are enjoying the sunshine and the green buds just barely showing on the green willow twigs. Virgil is sitting with his back against the tree trunk as he hopefully dangles his fishhook in the water of this lively little stream, the Maume River. I think Mac has settled us in here hoping for a fish fry for supper. This clear pool is made for a boy and his fishing line. I must not write all day for I've a sweater and socks to finish knitting, and I…

I may never finish that line. I was completely unprepared for the gasp followed by the great splash that was Virgil falling into that cold, deep pool. By the time I reached water's edge his head emerged, grim face straining to the surface, propelled forward by thrashing feet and wildly flailing arms. Aiding him too was the mild stream flow. I could not reach him, of course. To my relief and amazement I saw he was in no immediate need. He was swimming! In a moment he was standing on a sandbar rubbing the water from his face.

"Oh, Ma," he shouted, using the name he calls me when he is particularly elated. "I was swimming!"

"Yes, you were! But why…?" Before I could finish my question he was shivering vigorously. He waded through the shallow ripples to the shore.

Through chattering teeth he explained, "I didn't go to do it. I just leaned forward to see where that big fish went and I just slipped in. Did you see me swimming, Ma?" he asked, pulling off his wet sweater.

"Yes I did! You were swimming very well. Did you get wet?" I asked. I laughed while I quickly unfastened a petticoat and wrapped it around my shivering child.

"Oh, Ma, I can swim!" was his elated response.

CHAPTER 8

Fear of Water

Virgil's fall into the creek had a more pleasant ending than a fall I once had.

When I was 12 years old, Grandfather was driving our buggy across a rushing creek. I think Grandfather would have been more careful if Grandmother had been with us. She would have pointed out that the stream was swift and muddy, that it was not possible to see the best path for the wheels.

Nevertheless, the water was not at flood stage and was passable. The unexpected happened. A large boulder brushed against the buggy wheel. No spokes were broken but the wheel turned with unexpected speed and we lurched forward at such an angle that I was thrown out into the stream, landing on my back.

I had reached the adult age that permitted me to wear several petticoats. I must have had on all three that I owned for it was cold weather. Three wet petticoats dragged me down dangerously. I was floundering, flailing my arms frantically. I did not know how to swim. The swift flow was carrying me away toward the rear of the buggy. Grandfather yelled, "Grab the rear wheel!" That saved me.

No bones were broken, the bruises healed, but I never recovered from the fear of water. It has hovered with me always. As we have crossed the small streams on our journey they worried me, but only a bit, for I knew full well they were shallow. Mac, though he knows my fear, dismisses it as a senseless thing which I should get over and be done with.

Yesterday in crossing a river I felt an overwhelming urge to leave the wagon before it rolled onto the ferryboat. Of course I did no such thing. I gritted my teeth. I looked up to see if there were any clouds in the sky. Perhaps if I can always think of something unrelated to water I may eventually cure my problem. I suspect we will have enough streams to cross that I can try out my new idea.

At its bank the river lapped serenely. It looked miles across, but of course it was not. I told Mac that I planned to sit in the wagon and knit. He tersely agreed that I best do that.

I asked Virgil to come sit with me in the Conestoga. I knew he wished to be with his paw. I showed him he could watch the water better if he were sitting higher up in the wagon and we could sing some songs. I did not tell him the singing would keep me from hearing the water swish by. It is not a seemly thing to have him be aware of my fear. I would not want my dread to become settled in his mind.

CHAPTER 9

Morocco, Indiana to Kankakie, Illinois

April 3, 1865

We have traveled from home in Lima Ohio through Indiana to the Illinois State line in 33 days. It is a distance of 279 miles. I can scarcely believe we have come so far in only a month and two days. How well the teams have traveled!

The chill March wind has passed us now I hope. The weather is warming but it is still no hardship to spend the nights indoors at whatever stop we reach. So far Mac has planned for a restful night with a roof over our heads which has been good for man and beast.

Today is Mother's birthday. I posted her a letter two weeks ago. She may possibly have it by now. She will want to know all is well with us. Now that we are far apart I feel more closely drawn to both Mother and Father. I want them to know how much I appreciate the life they provided for Mac and me and for Virgil as he grew to be a big boy.

Our five-year-old boy is learning a bit of geography as we travel. From Ohio we have passed across Indiana. Now from Morocco, Indiana we will pass northerly through Illinois to cross the Mississippi River at Keokuk, Iowa. Mac is not certain yet where we will cross the Chariton River where the Clarks and the Bunselmeirs will take their leave of us.

That will be a sad parting. They have been such good companions and we have gained so much knowledge of good traveling from them.

CHAPTER 10

A Spring Storm

At first faint light this morning the dainty crescent moon, lighted by a single star, floated in the blue. Beneath it a massive black cloud filled the eastern sky. It was a beautiful sight but foreboding. We made short work of our host's hearty breakfast. As soon as we had packed food for the nooning, the three families of us stepped up into our wagons with hasty thanks and good-byes.

Our evening stop was a distant 20 miles. We could make it if all went well. The road, kept in good condition with dragging, was well drained and not slippery. The teams were restless and ready to be off.

Mac asked of Little Cloud, "Can we make 20 miles before nightfall?"

Little Cloud is brief with comments. He nodded. "Trail good. Travel fast. Teams know storm coming, Ready to go. We make it."

Mac turned his leather collar up against the steady wind and observed the storm could well be a nor'easter. I was grateful for warm leather clothing. The Bunselmeiers had guided us well on that score. A nor'easter is not to be anticipated with pleasure except for Virgil and Matthew. They were delighted when the stinging mist at nooning turned to a dry, fine snow. The storm was commencing.

I felt anxious. As the afternoon lengthened, I searched for something I could do to improve our situation. Somehow the silence increased the tension, even slowed the progress we must make before dusk. When we were not walking to keep warm, Virgil and I began singing softly. I was amazed at the difference. We felt a new lightness and cheer. Virgil chose "Tenting Tonight," "The Old Oaken Bucket," and "Jesus Loves Me."

It is well that we found our needed encouragement before we pulled up to the log cabin stop. We had five inches of snow already and the fine, dry flakes blew steadily.

No one came to greet us. There was a rude covered shelter for our four teams. The original barn had burned. The snow had scarcely covered the animal skeletons that remained. The men kicked the larger pieces of bone aside to make room for our wagons. I felt a pain of sorrow for these people who had suffered so great a loss, perhaps in an Indian raid.

The men fastened blankets over the steaming horses and went about their chores, Virgil and Matthew helping. We three woman went to the cabin. Again no one greeted us for no one was there. We returned to the wagon and agreed on what supplies we would need for the night and the morning start; beans, flour for gravy and biscuits at breakfast, but bacon, gravy and hot biscuits for supper. Two Dutch ovens to make biscuits, a skillet for frying, the teakettle and the table settings filled our needs.

How grateful we felt for the shelter. Although the fireplace did not draw well at first because of the storm, the chimney soon heated up and all went well. The 24-by-18-foot cabin, once someone's pride and joy, was now furnished with only a rude table made of a smoothed split log laid across bolts of firewood. I was sure there were no cobwebs festooned about when our absent hostess was in charge. Now the boys had a jolly time snagging the many webs down with split-wood brooms. Even the loft was not spared their activities.

The cabin was cozy and warm by the time we ate supper. Seated around the fireplace, on round chucks of firewood in place of stools, we had a jolly evening talking of the past day and relevant stories. The nodding heads of our tired boys gave us the good-night message. Their firewood chores had been finished in double amount in readiness for leave-taking on the morrow. Mac placed some choice sticks at either end of the fireplace to be well dried for the morning fire. I hung the bean pot just over the ash-covered coals to cook slowly through the night; the teakettle was placed nearby to keep warm and my chores were finished. We women slept in the warm loft and the men guarded the fire and the door below. We folded ourselves into our warm comforters for a good night's sleep.

Since the cabin had no windows we lighted a candle, but did not know the surprise that was in store for us. Mac tried to open the door. It did not budge. He and Little Cloud put their shoulders to it and with a mighty shove showed us a wondrous, white world outside. It was still snowing on top of the eighteen inches that lay smoothly drifted into four-foot hills wherever the wind chose to sculpt the scene.

Mac's first thought was to see to the horses. My first thought was to melt snow to make water for washing our clothing. Virgil and Matthew yelled, "We're snowbound! We're snowbound!," never thinking of the shoveling work ahead of them. The Bunselmeiers and the Clarks agreed that indeed we were snowbound for several days. They nodded their heads at the thought of the work to be done.

I hoped for some strong men to help with the clothes-wringing. More likely there were harnesses that needed mending or strengthening. No matter. The boys can help some. The clothes will freeze-dry easily.

CHAPTER 11

Snowbound Means Work

The boys were dressed in double time. They grabbed a cold biscuit, washed it down with a ready cup of tea and were all set for fun. The men stomped in and spoiled their plans.

"Too bad, boys! This fine dry snow is no good for making forts or snow-men. You'd have all that work for nothing. Those round balls would never stick together," pronounced Mac.

The boys' disappointment showed but Mac continued cheerfully. "The drifts are light-weight and make easy shoveling. So, let's get busy as soon as breakfast is over. Can't start a big job on an empty stomach."

Elijah Clark added, "Since the snow is dry and light I believe we men could fashion a drag that the horses could pull to clear our entry path out to the main trail. Tomorrow we could possibly start clearing that trail."

The other men nodded in agreement. The boys were looking at Winfield's whittling which he held up for inspection. What are you making?," questioned Virgil.

"These one-by-two-foot boards are not very wide," came the reply, "but I've whittled out some handholds in the handles so it will be easier for shovel work."

The boys grinned their pleasure and cheerfully thanked the young man for his thoughtfulness. It would be a good day after all.

We all sat down to bowls of mush, hot biscuits and gravy, and sugar in our tea. All of us hurried through the meal knowing what a lot of work lay ahead of us. Someone had thoughtfully supplied me with three buckets of snow which sat melting at the fire's edge.

After breakfast I asked Mac to bring in some beans, bacon and an onion. I surely disliked asking to be waited on in such a fashion but there was not yet a clear path out to the supply wagon. Of course he never minds being helpful, and he knows we'll have baked beans for supper.

The boys were soon out with their new shovels. We women stood in the doorway for just a minute to watch them throwing snow on each other. They laughed until they fell over, then started in earnest to clear out the path that was already begun by the men's footprints. The shovels were a great success.

I think Blanche Bunselmeier was half wishful she could be out with the boys. She came to me asking if it would be all right if she went out to the supply wagon for a cup of sugar and then she would make a cake for our noon meal.

I thought it a lovely plan. She found her leather boots and sallied forth. I think she and her husband had a little exchange of snowballs for she came in red-cheeked and laughing, but the sugar was well covered.

In about an hour Mac sent the boys in for a short rest and to warm up a bit. I took the hint and sent the boys out with a small bucket of hot tea for the men. It wouldn't hurt them to all share the same bucket since there was no other way. The boys came back in chasing one another and laughing.

Matthew was saying, "No, you cannot beat me at checkers." Virgil, of course, disagreed.

"We can make a playing board on your shovel. It's wider than mine and we can mark the squares with charcoal," urged Virgil. "And we can use some of the whittlings for the pieces. I'll put a black dot on mine."

In no time there was a serious checker game going on, a cake was baking at the hearth, Catherine and I were washing and rinsing clothes, and the men were busy making a road-drag for the horses to pull. Snowbound, indeed! We might as well be home in Lima, Ohio as almost to Keokuk, Iowa on the Mississippi River. Life goes on much the same. But the snowstorm I do regret.

CHAPTER 12

At the Chariton River Crossing

Crossing the broad and swift-moving Mississippi River at Keokuk on board a paddle wheeler gave us a deal less trouble than crossing this smaller, swollen Chariton River. The thaws have come early and the feeder streams, flooded with the winter snows, swirl into the river's broken chunks of ice piled along the edge. These piles grind away the banks and the river rushes forward flooding into nearby fields.

While we wait for wind and sun to dry the land the men are busy baling slag with hog wire that will later be used to give a firm footing on the river banks. Of course rocks are scarce as hen's teeth in this fine Missouri soil, but the nearby coal mine gives us all the slag we need just for hauling it away. Slag is a rough and hard rock-like cinder.

The river men know ahead of time they will have a need for such and get their slag bundles ready early. Drawing them on a sled to the river when the ground is frozen is less troublesome. We have come too late for that so will make a trade with the river men. With what we have bundled at the mine, plus a few coins, we will dicker for what they have already hauled to the river for use. The bundles are placed on the river bank to prevent the wagon wheels from sinking in to the hubs.

The black-mudded Chariton River glowered as it flowed before us. I pushed the hair from my forehead hoping I could see better. It seemed a mile from bank to bank though we plainly saw the pulleymen guiding the emptied ferry boats toward us. Our turn for loading was at hand. My heart was pounding, and as Virgil might have said, "my innards didn't feel so good." Perhaps we should not load on.

Virgil did not think this, only his fearful mother. Indeed, Virgil could not wait to board. To him the silent rushing water was not an evil thing of violent strength, relentless in claiming all that ventured into its eddying, swaying mass of ice and huge chunks of mud.

The ferry bumped to the loading dock. In a moment the boatman was firmly steadying my entrance on board.

"Watch your step," he commanded.

Only then did I realize my eyes had been closed against this fearful entry to the watery world. With eyes wide opened, I watched only my feet. Virgil held my hand that carried my knitting basket.

I felt safe. The people were urged to the port side while the wagons were carefully rolled starboard, had their wheels removed and stored within their load.

When our boat surged into the open stream I quietly slipped a light yarn over my wrist and snugged the other over Virgil's hand.

"Thank you, Mama," he said quietly. "Now that I can swim I can pull you to shore if we land in the water."

He smiled at me knowingly. I smiled back but found I could not speak, realizing with a swell of pride I was in the protective care of this five-year-old young man.

CHAPTER 13

The Winding Missouri River

Like a monster, the great Missouri River swallows all the streams, large or small, that cross its path. To make certain it has missed none it curls back along its forward path in tortuous winding, searching for strays. Virgil says even a giant walking across the land would splash with every step into the mighty meandering river. It keeps a constant check on where it has been and has little care for where it flows.

We have hurried to cross the great river before flood time. Traveling as we do some distance from its curving form, we see evidence of its high flood-water marks far inland from its banks. What a great threat it must be to the towns and farms along its way. If we can arrive at the crossing before the winter snows are melted we will have little trouble. If we have to wait for the water level to become safe for crossing it means there will be much crowding. Many people and their animals will be milling about waiting, waiting. We will have to wait to see how the weather deals with us.

At some flood times the river has not always returned to its old streambed but has made a new curve, a new nest to comfort itself. The old curve is left forever stranded a distance away. This oxbow may keep its water for awhile, even be useful to the farmer until it begins to dry up, leaving the land too wet to farm and too dry in summer for crops. The oxbow appears smooth and inviting to cross. Smooth it is, but treacherous whether of dry, fine soil or thick, sucking mud.

We entered just such a muddy area today. When we had driven in only a few feet the mules stopped, sensing they should travel no farther. We were caught in a trap. Putting our shoulders to the wagon we pried and pushed. We were in greater peril than at the muddy Chariton River crossing and we had fewer men to help. Out of breath and exhausted, how we longed for the help of Little Cloud or the Bunselmeiers. I thought we were about to abandon our worldly goods. Mac put down the third plank and we edged first one then another of the barrels along it to a safe spot. Even this was not easy as we slithered about in the mud. Only Virgil thought it was fun. After the rest and the lightened load the mules strained mightily and we were out free. But what a mud-encased mess we all were. When we reached the next stream even Mac helped with scrubbing our clothes. Virgil did not think this kind of mud play was much fun.

Since crossing the Chariton, the Yellow, and the Grand Rivers that flow southerly, we have driven closer to the Missouri's north bank. It has been easy travel and inns are plentiful along the way. Oft' times there were other children Virgil could play with. Most of the travelers were bound for Oregon or California. We learned of none who are headed for Arizona Territory. Mac says that is good for he has no wish to travel each day in a mile-long procession of animals and wagons. I suppose I will not be lonely but it is pleasant to have other women about. I do miss the Clarks and the Bunselmeiers since they left us at Kirksville, Missouri.

CHAPTER 14

Virgil Lost

I am completely distraught and sick with worry. We do not know where Virgil is. It is not his way to leave us and wander about. Someone has taken the child. He is held against his will, I am convinced. In this over-crowded inn we have separate sleeping quarters. Mac and Virgil are in the men's area. It never occurred to us the child needed to be guarded against kidnappers. With each passing hour the situation seems more serious. Mac has been gone, searching for him, all morning.

When last seen Virgil was with his father in the crowded eating hall of long tables where the men were being fed first. Mac was discussing the river crossing with the gentleman on his right. Virgil was having a friendly conversation on the left with a young man. All Mac knows is the men said he runs a supply boat across the Missouri River every day.

I think it is to our good luck he cannot now cross. No one can. The river is dangerously high and out of its banks, else we would not be waiting here. If the young man has taken Virgil off with him, these days of rain are a Godsend. They may give us time to find the child. I must find a way to be of good courage, but I am worried sick. I cannot concentrate, even to read the Bible.

For three days we, and I think half of the world, have been waiting here on the western edge of the Missouri at St. Joseph in a steady downpour. We are fortunate our inn has a room for women, though we are sleeping across the bed, four to a bed.

I do not mind the temporary arrangement and there is no other place to go. The room is almost filled with the bed and chair. We place our clothing in a neat pile under the bed. My companion is a woman 15 years my senior who has her two daughters of 12 and 14 with her. They are quiet, pleasant people and and the room is clean with no sign of bedbugs. Who knows when even this may change. There are precautions taken against the bugs for the smell of kerosene is strong and the bed joints are wet with recent treatment.

My mind is constantly with Mac and his search. When he missed Virgil, the child could have been gone only a minute or two. He searched the eating hall, asked the serving girl, then stepped outside to look up and down the busy street. He inquired of a group of men about a young man and a little boy. There were conflicting reports on which direction they took and whether they crossed the street. They did agree that the two had come out the door for Virgil's happy expression had been remembered. Mac came to my room, to keep me informed, then sped away with real concern on his face.

There is nothing I can do but wait and worry. I should go to the kitchen and give some help. I can peel potatoes or knead bread. Any job will help to keep my mind busy until Mac's return. I pray to our Heavenly Father for His watchful care and safe return of my two men.

CHAPTER 15

A Cure for Worry

Mac had been gone for some time before I realized I had eaten no breakfast. Food was not important; only finding Virgil. I truly had no idea what I could do but eating was not one of them. Listening for footsteps to stop at my door became unbearable. I decided I would go to the kitchen, find some busy work, then perhaps some thought would come to me.

Carefully I made certain my money was well pinned inside my clothing, stepped out the bedroom door, walked down the hallway to a window and gazed down below. I was amazed. The streets below were crowded with activity. In both directions whips snaked out over six-horse teams pulling wagonloads of goods. The wagon wheels were mired to their hubs in mud.

Every driver was trying to hurry past the plodding oxteams that mingled in the overcrowded road. The ruts prevented their passing and increased the drivers' ire. My heart sank thinking of Virgil out there alone and trying to cross such a dangerous street filled with sharp hoofs, rolling wheels and ruts that could swallow him up. On the boardwalk throngs were passing, paying mind to no one.

How could our little boy survive out there alone? How could he find his way back to us? How can we know where to look for him? I felt so helpless but I would not let the tears come. Weeping would be of no help whatsoever.

I turned and started to the kitchen. Certainly they would be glad to have someone peel potatoes for the next meal to feed all these stranded, hungry people.

The first person I saw in the busy, steamy kitchen was an old lady surely as Scottish as my own dear Granny. I smiled and did not know what an effort it would take.

"May I help you peel potatoes, Ma'am?," I invited myself and reached for a paring knife.

Her warm smile moved me. "Aye, lass. Call me Maude. There's work aplenty. These gnarled old hands welcome ye. Sure now and what heavy burden hangs over ye?"

I swallowed hard to control my voice and speak like a lady but found I could not speak at all. The dear soul had completely disarmed me with her gentle understanding before I had even spoken.

"There, there, now think on it a bit." She was so like Granny I nearly folded her in my arms. My anguished tale poured from me.

She clucked in deep dismay and concern, patted my hand and assured me everything would turn out all right.

"Oh, thank you," I began, "but those throngs of people out there, the wagons, the deep muddy ruts. If Virgil ever slipped and fell…"

"Don't ye be a frettin'," she coaxed. "There's many a body lookin' for ye'r wee bairn. My grandson Scott is a hearty mon and a constable, too, he is. Ye may be assured he'll be a helpin'. We will nay be seein' him until nicht. If virgil be not safe in ye'r arms this day, ye will clasp him to ye'r bosom on the morrow."

I scarcely believed my burden was already lighter. We finished the cauldron of potatoes. Then I realized I was hungry. Friend, Maude, and I arranged a meeting place at the great dining room clock. I set forth to eat a delayed breakfast.

After serving my plate with chunks of potatoes and gravy, a fat sausage, and cornbread with fresh churned butter, I sat alone, bowed my head and asked a most fervent blessing on us all.

CHAPTER 16

A Child's Cry for Help

When I had finished my late meal I noticed the clock on the mantel was ready to strike eleven. Best I return to my room, I thought, in case Mac came looking for me. To my surprise we met at the foot of the staircase. He had already been to the room but had no news to report, though he had been all around the three city blocks that bordered on our inn.

Mac wanted me to return to our room and get some rest. He said I looked haggard. He planned to eat then go looking on the waterfront for Virgil. The thought that our child might have drowned had never entered my mind. Now I'm certain I must have taken on a haggard look.

I was ready to pull down the window shade and get some rest when I heard a child's voice, a scream, really. I peered out the tiny bedroom window but could not see below me. Across the street there were no children in sight nor did any of the people over there seem to be staring toward my side of the street.

I snatched up my shawl and ran from the room without taking time to lock up. I entered the dining room in a most unladylike fashion. "Mac!" I called sharply and motioned for him to come. We both rushed ourt while I was explaining about the cry I had heard. When we arrived in the alley, at the south side of the building below my window, there was no one in sight, no one we could ask questions of. We looked behind the trees. I even peered up among the bare branches. We tried every entry door to the inn and found them locked. We called Virgil's name, all to no avail. We felt completely defeated, but of course it was only a slim chance that it was our boy calling. I think Mac thought I was hearing things.

We returned to the inn, Mac to eat and I to try lying down again. As I went to the window there was a repeat of a child's scream. This time I took a careful look all around. There truly was nothing to be seen. The building across the alley had a window open and a ragged curtain flying out. I could see nobody, nor a child beyond the window. An open window was nothing unusual. The Dutch housekeepers were forever with their windows open and curtains or bedding hanging out. Even a heavy rain did not prevent the airing of the house. I returned to my bed. I was truly weary.

CHAPTER 17

Fault

As I lay on the bed I began to realize there was an anger growing in my heart. Yes, an anger toward the man who had snatched our little boy, but an anger toward Mac, too, that he had been so engrossed in the stranger on his right that he had forgotten all about his son on his left. Then the thought came to my mind, Mac blames me, too, for being so unwilling to join him at the breakfast table because the room was filled with only men. I had made it clear that a swearing mob of tobacco-chewing men was no place for a lady. Or for a young boy, either. The boy of course stayed with his paw. Mac is so afraid I'll make too much of a gentleman of Virgil.

Oh, I realized in anguish, this is no time to be casting blame. No one is at fault except the wicked man who stole our child. I was close to weeping again and I could not sleep. I went to the window and raised the sash to look below.

At the end of the alley was a privy I had not notice before. It was a large one with two doors. Someone started to pass from one doorway then returned within. Again a foot appeared then was withdrawn. Just as I closed the sash the foot appeared a third time. I also noticed something seemed to be protruding from the moon window in the same door. I could not see what the object was but thought it an ordinary situation of a mother restraining her child.

I turned from the window and made myself ready to meet with Maude at the old clock downstairs. I found Mac waiting there and recounted the scene at the privy. Of course he knew about the privy but I could see he was thinking of meeting with the constable and how Maude could direct us.

She came slowly, walking painfully. With her warm smile she greeted us, "Aye, and I see ye have brought Mac- 'Tis pleased to make your acquaintance, Oiy am."

Mac led her to a seat and began to gather information on how to meet her grandson, Scott, the constable. She explained all, then added that there was a gang of thieves working the busy river crossing who were stealing all they could lay hand to, even small boys who were put to service as virtual slaves as cabin boys or as roust-a-bouts. Again she encouraged us that Virgil would be found shortly for her burly grandson could manage these devil-men and had a constant eye on their doings.

Before Mac hurried off to find Scott on his rounds out on the street, we three agreed to meet at six, under the clock, for supper. Under my breath I prayed, "May the good Lord allow Mac to bring Virgil with him, too."

CHAPTER 18

The Search

Maude and I turned to the kitchen entry. I asked if she thought it would be all right for me to find some busy work with her. "I could slice bread, churn butter, make gravy or any such little thing," I suggested. Maude patted my shoulder and assured me I was welcome to come in and keep occupied. Then, almost as an afterthought, she added, "My family owns the Inn. 'Tis happy I am to have your company." Then she laughed heartily at my surprise.

We talked as we worked together slicing long loaves of bread. I happened to mention the scene I'd watched out the window earlier. Maude showed considerable interest and remarked that the thieves had at one time used one side of the privy to stow their loot, thinking it an unlikely place to be searched.

"Oh," I gasped, "could it possibly be a stolen child held there? That it was not just a mother and her child?" I laid down my knife and made ready to go to the alley.

"Aye, now Lassie," cautioned Maude, "Ye kenna nay do this thing alone. Ye may nay come back alive. They are wicked and desperate men. Come, from my room we can watch. The woodman can be sent to fetch Scott, the constable. We'll be gettin' to the bottom of this, but we must have the law and some burly men to bring it off properly."

Maude and I were in her sitting room and had a clear view of the door where I'd seen the foot appear. The moon window was stuffed with a piece of gunny sack, a bit of it dangling in the breeze. It did seem most likely that something strange was happening. How I longed to go yank that door open or pound on it and scream for Virgil to come out. But of course Maude was right.

We simply could not do this thing alone. I must sit quietly and keep a close watch. This was surely the most difficult thing I had ever done in my life.

Maude sent the serving girl from the dining room to fetch Jake for her. She had no need of wood but sent him on an errand to find Scott, the constable. There was a need to search the privy again. Jake realized the importance of his message.

CHAPTER 19

Release

In about half an hour after the constable was called we saw old Jake, the wood-man, slip up quietly toward the privy, finger at lips. Behind him stepped a burly Scotsman, red beard sparkling in the mist. Next came Mac, teamed up with the Scotsman. Then I realized all three were armed with guns. Supplied by the constable. We could not hear the voices but their stance told us much.

Scott was speaking and a demand was made of whoever was inside the darkened little building. The door opened a very little. One small boy squeezed out, not Virgil at first, but a taller, red-haired boy. Another demand was made by Scott and the other child squeezed through the slit in the door. There had been two boys! Both had their fists in their eyes rubbing out the bright light of day. I would have known that tousled towhead of Virgil's anywhere. I wanted to run out and gather him in my arms but Maude knew this was not the time. I restrained myself and softly breathed, "Praise the Lord they both are alive and safe." Next came the childrens' abductor. The men manacled his arms behind his back. Then while he sat in the privy doorway, they manacled his feet and jerked him up to be led away.

I did not see his face nor did I want to see it. I could see Virgil now, huddled with the other boy at Mac's feet—a safe place and out of harm's way but I longed to hold him again. The tears were now streaming down my face until I scarce could see.

Scott and Old Jake were taking the thief away. His mincing, manacled steps were ludicrous, but I was not the least entertained as were the children who came from nowhere to laugh and point in derision. Maude showed me to the door and I ran out into the alley to gather those two little boys in my arms. Their fast beating hearts told me they had been through a day of dreadful fright.

CHAPTER 20

Safe

Virgil flung his arms about my neck and cried, "Mama, oh, Mama!"

The other little boy began to withdraw from the embrace of a stranger, but I patted him on the back and asked him his name.

"Willie," he answered hoarsely. "Willie Sturgis. My paw is a blacksmith and he's gonna give that man, Ram, an awful beatin' if'n he ever shows up at the forge again. He's a mean man."

"Mama," began Virgil, "he was mean. He locked us in the privy. Then he was gonna tie Willie and I grabbed at the rope on the floor and that man stomped on my hand and he shoved me and I fell down and he said…" At this point Virgil began to sob, then he stopped and continued. "He said he would throw me in the toilet if I did that again."

Virgil could say no more but cried quietly as we walked into Maude's room where she had milk and cookies waiting.

"Yes, he did," agreed Willie, choosing a large sugar cookie. "And then he tied up Virgil, too." Angrily Willie explained, "Me and paw thought Ram was our friend. I knowed my paw wouldn't care none if we went to see Ram's boat. But Ram never took us to see the boat ner nothin' like that. After we had walked a long way he took us to the privy, tied us up and locked us in. I told him we wanted to go home and I knowed the way if he'd just let us out. He just stuffed the moon window full with a gunny sack and told us we better shut up if we knowed what was good for us. And he said he'd take us to the boat after dark. We didn't want to go then. He was too mean."

"He was mean," Virgil added again.

Willie continued, "It was so dark we couldn't see much, but when Ram began to snore in his sleep I stuck my foot out at the bottom of the door, but I couldn't make it open. Then Ram woke up and hit me. As long as he didn't do more than hit me I kept tryin'. When I tell my paw he ain't gonna like Ram no more." Willie sniffed quietly, kept back the sobs and wiped his wet face on his shirt sleeve.

"Willie," said Mac, reaching out his hand toward the boy, "I want to thank you for taking care of Virgil while you were out there today. You were a fine young man and did everything just right. We are sorry we didn't find you sooner."

"Oh, sir," replied the youngster earnestly, "I didn't take care of Virgil. We took care of each other. He pulled my shirt sleeves down under the ropes so it wouldn't hurt so much. And we agreed not to cry 'cause that just made Ram madder and he would hit us some more."

How my heart ached for those two little boys. Their agony had been far greater than ours. "Thank you, Lord," I breathed, "thank you, thank you. They are safe at least from that evil man."

Willie had more to say. "Virgil told me not to be skeered 'cause you would find us even if we couldn't get out. My paw is sure gonna be powerful proud of you, sir."

Mac explained about Scott, the constable, and how all of us helped. "Your paw might be wondering about you," Mac suggested. "I'm glad you can show me the way."

Stalwart little Willie slipped his hand into Mac's, said goodbye to me, Virgil and Maude, accepted a few proffered cookies and moved off to show Mac the way to the smithy's before dark set in. What a day this has been.

I wanted to hold Virgil and rock him like a three-year-old. I was so deeply happy to have my child back again, but we sat together on Maude's settee, my arm about his shoulders, while he haltingly repeated the story of his frightful day.

Of course that wicked man lied to the child to get him to leave Mac. Virgil had been told that he had permission to go with Ram to see the boat. On the street the two met Willie, who knew Ram, and went willingly. Both boys realized their mistake later but too late to break free.

When Virgil had talked the story out I realized he was still too upset to have cookies or milk. I remarked that we should go upstairs and put on clean dry clothes before supper. I thanked Maude heartily and told her surely the good Lord had directed us to meet.

As Virgil and I moved toward the stairs, people turned and stared after us. I did not tell my child that he still smelled of the privy.

CHAPTER 21

On Watch

Mac returned from the smithy's before dark, reporting that Willie surely knew his way about town and used several shortcuts to his home. Mr. Sturgis, taken aback that his son had been in such danger, was most grateful for the lad's return. To Mac he gave assurance that should there be anything we needed for our journey it would be forthcoming. Mac will go to Mr. Sturgis' forge tomorrow and the two of them will plan what beasts will be best suited for the journey ahead.

Mac ate supper with us then departed to spend the night in our covered wagon. Sleeping at the inn would be more comfortable than a buffalo-robe bed in the wagon but there are quilts aplenty for warmth. The constable told Mac to stay on guard. It is the only way to make certain our goods are not plundered in the night. The rain has stopped and except for that evil Ram, who is behind bars, thieves will be out looking for unguarded treasure. We must not chance losing our gear and supplies.

Since the three who shared my bed have moved on, there is room for Virgil to sleep with me. We may have another roomer with us yet tonight, though I hope not. I will sleep poorly enough with Virgil's moving about.

Next Morning

True to my surmise, as soon as Virgil had settled into a deep sleep, the chambermaid came knocking. A weary traveler needed the other half of my bed. She disturbed us very little. I had prepared for such a happening and already had tied a strip of cloth from my ankle to Virgil's. I did not want anyone lifting the child from the bed whilst I slept. I suppose Mac will laugh about it but I mean to keep our child safe.

We spent a quiet night except for Virgil crying out once in his dreams.

CHAPTER 22

Scallawags on Board

I was the first to step aboard to cross the Missouri River. That meant I would have longer to wait before the gangplank was taken up, but it also meant I would have a longer time to compose myself for this fearful trip, coward that I am when on the water.

This was the largest flatboat I had been on and I felt it to be the most stable. The wagons had first been lined up in the center. All wheels were removed and the front ones loaded in at the driver's seat. The back ones, inside the load, leaned against the barrels in the rear of the wagon. Our wheels were newly tired and in tiptop condition for the long journey ahead. They stood properly placed, all safe from "unauthorized exchanges." I felt secure sitting near our wagon bed. Since the kidnapping and recovery of Virgil I find it difficult to trust anyone now.

All the animals had been herded on the starboard of the wagons, and hobbled in place. The wagons made a good and safe separation of animals and people. The men stayed with their teams. Virgil and his paw were with our new team of oxen. Mac decided to buy the oxen on the Missouri side of the river to have a better chance of getting a good dependable yoke than when we landed in Kansas.

Such a hubbub! People milling about, babies crying, children calling, their mothers calling them. Finally the passengers and all the possessions they could carry had been loaded on the port side of the ferry. All odors blew downwind from us. We hoped it would last.

I felt more at ease than I had in any other river crossing. It is well I did, for this Missouri River trip was to be a much longer ordeal. The water level was yet high and flowing with great speed. I chose not to watch the swirling eddies cut great chunks of mud from the bank. They slid like black demons out of sight under the mighty current, never to reappear.

I did not allow Virgil near the boat's edge, where he delighted in watching the destruction. He was under his Paw's watchful eye

Had I not heard the clang of the gangplank I would not have noticed we had slipped from our mooring and were entering the mainstream. I kept busy with my knitting, glad that the hum of people's voices, and the animals' whinnying and lowing sounds drowned out the threat of the rushing water.

We were nearing the opposite shore when a man and woman approached me. She politely introduced herself and her husband as Mrs. and Mr. Brown, and asked if my name might be Mrs. McGinnis. I smiling assured her it was. Then her husband said he had a message from my husband. I was to go over to Mac right away and Mrs. Brown would show me the way.

Right off, I thought there was something wrong with Virgil. I quickly stuffed my knitting away and was ready to go. We had walked the length of two wagons when I thought to look back to get my bearings for when I should return. There to my startled eyes was Mr. Brown stepping into our wagon, one hand already rolling out one of our wheels.

"Stop him! Stop him!," I screamed. "That is not his wagon wheel! Help! Help!"

Mr. Brown, if that was his name, dropped the wheel as he made a mad dash to the wagon's front, leaped out and was lost in the crowd. I turned about to look for Mrs. Brown but she had performed a disappearing act as well. With all the noise about I think no one really saw or knew what had happened.

I returned the short distance to our wagon and gathered myself together. I determined I would step from the ferry with that wagon under my very close watch. The idea! Those scallawags stealing things right from under my nose! And a woman helper too!

CHAPTER 23

The Friend's Picture

May, 1865

Dearest Mother and Father,

We trust you are well and have seen the beginning of a good summer. If you received my last letter you know we have made that fearful crossing of the broad, flooded Missouri River. We thank the dear Lord for our safety.

I must tell you of a very strange incident that introduced us to the booming state of Kansas. We had found our night's lodging on the west side of Parkville, Kansas, in readiness for an early start next morning. Outside our inn's doorway a nicely dressed gentleman, complete with a natty bowler hat, stopped us and politely gained our attention. He asked Mac if we would like to have our photographs made.

Well, you may be certain I was not interested in any shenanigans offered by a stranger. After that incident of the scalawags trying to steal our newly tired wheels while on the river crossing, I find I have little faith in strangers. But Mac, somehow, seemed curious enough to ask to see a sample of his work.

You will find it hard to believe what he showed us. It was a picture of my friend Mary Haw who left Lima, Ohio three years before we left for Arizona Territory. Truly it was a good likeness of both her and her husband, Joseph. Her baby has grown to be a big boy of about three. Her brother, home from the War of Northern Aggression, as he names the Rebellion, was wearing a gunbelt of large bullets and carrying a modern short-bar-reled rifle.

But what took my eye especially was Mary wearing her silk wedding dress with its broad brown stripes. You may remember she made it in such a fashion that the stripes of the sleeves turned in serpentine twists from the shoulder to the wrist. Of course she wore the beautiful leather gloves her uncle had sent her from Italy. All the members of the picture held their hats in their hands so I did not determine whether Mary had a new bonnet or had refurbished hers.

They were all standing near a covered wagon pulled by a fine looking team of horses and were on their way to Oregon, so said our photographer art-ist. I could scarcely believe my eyes and ears.

The canvas sides of their Prairie Schooner had been raised to reveal the interior. And, Mother, there in plain sight was the birds-eye-maple wash-stand which we gave her as a wedding gift! It was strapped securely in place to the wagon bed with one set of legs placed on the outside. They are truly traveling in high style. We wash from a tin basin!

I must post this in the next postbag going East. Farewell for now. We send you both our love. May God keep us all in His loving care.

Molly

P.S. We did not have our picture made! Such a frivolous thing we could not afford.

CHAPTER 24

Snake Encounter

Today was another long hot day of travel. I am weary. Dear Father urged me not to consider such a long journey from Lima, Ohio to Arizona Territory. But go I would, arguing that the trail was much more civilized now in 1865.

It was clear I knew much about false reports. We left civilized country months ago when we made that terrifying crossing of the flooded Missouri

River at St. Joseph. That was in April. Since then, in two months, we have passed four houses, or sod huts. Kansas Territory is sparsely settled.

Two weeks ago we stopped at a sod hut at the noon rest. Ah, the sole occupant was a weary, disillusioned soul. Had we but asked her she would have joined us. Anything looked better to her and we are no prize. She tucked her hair under her frumpy sunbonnet and then kindly gave us a squash she had picked from her garden. Fresh vegetables are a welcome change. I gave her a cup of sugar and two cups of flour to make a cake. Her smile lightened our day as we hurried on our way.

It has been hazy and humid, but not burning hot. So, except for our noon rest and our hourly five-minute rest, we have traveled the whole day; Mac said over fifteen miles. The sun was nearing the horizon when we found a most suitable camp spot with cottonwood trees and a lively little stream.

The burbling sound of that moving water made me want to sit in the shade and dally awhile. But there was the fire to start and tend, and close tending it will need with this tall grass about us. I warned Virgil not to go down the slight bank to the stream for I'd be needing him shortly. Of course he stood and watched the flowing water but minded what I had said. He had a long staff in his hand and walked about, no doubt pretending to be some traveler giving camp directions.

Mac was tending the oxen, giving them a rub down and a part of their rations. He and Virgil would take them to the stream later when they had cooled down from their day's work.

I was startled when I heard Mac sternly command, "Don't move, Virgil."

I looked immediately toward the child. He was stirring something in the grass with his long stick. When my gaze shifted to Mac he was pointing his gun toward Virgil's feet. I stifled a scream.

The rifle shot thundered in the stillness and echoed from the distant horizon. Coils of a writhing snake were flung about Virgil's feet. Then I did scream, "Virgil! Come here this instant!"

By then the child gladly jumped away from the contorted thrashing of the dead but revolting snake. Mac carefully advanced a few steps to have a look around. There might be another varmint traveling with the one he had shot.

I must admit I was not thinking of such precautions. I grabbed Virgil by the shirt sleeve, pulled him to me, flung him over my checkered red apron and soundly spanked him several licks, shouting all the while, "Don't you ever poke at a snake again!"

With that I came to my senses. I set the child upon his feet as my voice returned to normal. I continued to admonish him about the dangerous thing he had done, playing with a snake! Through his snuffles and tears he tried to explain that it was all curled up and he thought it was dead.

"No matter," I sternly commanded, "leave him alone. If he is dead or even a good snake, leave him alone. And if he is a bad snake you have no business poking at him, dead or alive. Now, tell me, what do you do with a snake?"

"Leave him alone," he mumbled, with all the joy gone from his day.

Mac joined us, put his hand on Virgil's shoulder and asked firmly, "Did you hear what your mother said?"

"Yes, Papa," came the serious reply.

Mac had more to say. "Virgil, I want you to know this, too. You were a very brave boy to obey me and not move. That snake was ready to strike you if you had made a motion. I had to blow his head off with no time to lose."

"Come, if you are not needed at the fire right now you can help me bury what is left of the head. He was a big prairie rattler and the head must not be left lying about. The poison in it is dangerous to any living creature. You may have the rattles. They are a fine trophy and not at all poisonous. We'll throw the body in the stream. Your Maw would not abide having its skin hanging about, and I reckon we have enough food, we don't need to eat snake meat."

As the two moved away I heard Virgil say, "I'm glad you always carry the rifle slung on your back, Paw." Virgil slipped his hand into Mac's. All was right with the world again, and Virgil began talking about the snake's rattles.

CHAPTER 25

Trouble and Trouble

Yesterday we were sorely tried to rescue our newly purchased, though pitiful, worldly goods. So much was at stake we persevered almost beyond our endurance. To be turned back to Independence, Missouri was unthinkable and certainly not back to Ohio. Crossing that swirling Missouri River is something I'll never do again.

Our problem began because of our accomplishment two days before. By dint of great effort we had passed a large driven herd of cattle. The dirt and stench in traveling in the rear of them was unendurable. It was not the first time we had angered drovers by passing them. We traveled in a great semi-circle from them, carefully keeping well to their left. It was the only way to avoid frightening and perhaps stampeding the herd.

We urged our beasts on all day making more than twenty miles, Mac said. Passing is one thing, keeping well ahead is of vital importance. If by chance the cattle should be stampeded at night we could be in mortal danger of suddenly being trampled.

We traveled on late into the evening. It was a better plan than we knew. We rested well all night and were off earlier than our usual dawn departure, remembering well the stench from the herd of bawling cattle. Happily, they do travel more slowly than we do.

The noon rest stop was kept short in the meager shade at a dry creek bed. Immediately following our pleasant stop, when crossing to the far bank, we became lodged on a sand-covered bar of rock. Though the creek was not flowing the sand was moist. The front wheels sank to the hub in the wet sand as soon as they passed over the great rock.

There the wagon bed rested, on a ridge. The back wheels could not lift us up over such an impediment. We were stuck. Prying was not successful for our load was too heavy.

We were in a bed of moist quicksand and had to move entirely out of the stream bed. Indeed, every barrel must be moved fifty yards across the stream and up onto the bank.

How we did work! Virgil helped, too. He carried bucket after bucket of food to an empty keg to lighten the weight of the barrels. Beans were his favorite burden.

Mac lashed four poles together lengthwise. A barrel laid on its side carried very well on this litter. One needed only the strength to lift it between the oxen which then plodded to the far bank.

My need for rest became more and more frequent. Finally Mac ordered me to lie down. When I closed my eyes my limbs felt compelled to move. Momentarily I fell asleep and dreamed I was still walking that rough creek bed.

On waking my heart had stopped pounding. My head felt near to bursting. I tied a wet cloth tightly about my throbbing headache and went back to work.

Eventually we pried the wagon loose, aided by the oxen hitched to the rear axle. We were freed of our predicament. Then came the reloading of the wagon on the far bank. All went well.

We had diminished our head start by four hours. Even so there was no approaching herd or their dust in sight. There was some daylight traveling yet in the afternoon. We had succeeded.

By supper I had had enough rest. I was able to hold the spoon to stir the stew. Rested I was, but still did not feel like dancing a jig.

Virgil reported, "Once during our moving I thought that if only I should slip or stumble then I could sit and rest a bit. Just then you told me to take a rest, Paw. But you never rested. You must be very tired."

Mac, who never complains, smiled and remarked, "I'll get rested tonight."

CHAPTER 26

Fire Protection on the Prairie

Mac says he smells smoke. That means a prairie fire in the distance. Tonight we may see the sky lighted at the horizon. We have little wind here at present so it will be favorable to burn a fire break about our camp. Now we will stop earlier than usual and may travel less than ten miles today. The beasts will welcome the rest but I yearn to press on. I say little of the tiresome toil of the journey except to tell Mac of my gratitude to him. It is the driver who bears the brunt of the labor. Virgil and I can leave the wagon to get a rest. Mac walks usually in a special emergency for guiding the beasts through a mire or leading them through a difficult stream crossing. I wonder if Mac has ever regretted making this westward decision. I know I'll never admit aloud that it is a far greater trial than I had ever expected. I must dwell on it no longer.

After the noon break we began seeing more animals and birds. They are fleeing the distant prairie fire. We will have plenty of meat for supper.

We stopped in mid-afternoon to begin the fire control protection. The oxen were hitched to the plowshare to turn up a 50-foot circle of sod about our camp. It was a difficult job. The soil is dry and the matted grass is almost impossible to penetrate. Once started, the plowing seemed a bit easier on man and beast.

With the sod-turned circle protecting us, the firing began. Virgil was excited but calmed down when he saw how carefully protected we were. The oxen, now at liberty, but on a tether, were anxious at first, but soon turned warily to feeding on the tall grass within our enclosure. Mac began the fire circle about

100 yards out from the broken sod. Once the outer circle, two yards wide, was burned without mishap I know we all breathed easier.

It is a back-breaking job to keep the fire within bounds yet keep it burning. This one firebreak would have been sufficient, but Mac was more thorough.

Next came the burning of an inner circle 50 yards out from the sod circle. We staked the oxen outside the distant burn. They rested more quietly.

Between the two burned circles, small strips were burned. Virgil said they looked like wheel spokes. The spokes keep a fire from growing into a great firestorm. A prairie fire can move mighty fast. Anything we burn now avoids a great fire that would burn up the air, even within our protected camp.

With all the care taken there were moments now and then that taxed our efforts to keep the burning under control. Lighting smaller areas at a time also lessened the heat we felt. A great bonfire in the middle of June is no pleasure.

The smoke from the fire was mostly avoidable but the black ash from the burned grass was everywhere. To prevent tracking it about is impossible. Such a mess. I hope to wash our clothes soon. When we cross another creek I hope it is flowing.

Tonight the western sky flares red and pales only at the zenith. It is red enough to convince one that Hell itself is just over the horizon. I must mind my language but what else could be said?

Mac feels certain he has us well protected. The oxen were led docilely into our safe camp. At supper they munched the dry grass. We had prairie chicken. I cooked enough for the next day though there will be no dumplings then. In the long rest this afternoon I set some bread dough, and baked it later this evening. Virgil and I stepped lively to keep the right amount of twisted grass for a slow, baking fire.

We rise early to rid ourselves of a restless night. I am not certain I sleep. Mac tosses and turns the night through. That black circle of burned grass is a comfort against fire danger but we feel a need to be alert. With Mac's encouraging words the wagons pull out before sunup. We track the blackened grass in and on the wagon, an unsightly mess! The harsh burned smell would be behind us, so I thought. The breeze quickened in the late afternoon to bring a fresh scent but not for our clothes. They will have to be washed. We cannot come to a creek too soon. I would even wash on the Sabbath. Surely God in His mercy is understanding.

Rain threatened, again none fell. The cloud cover is always welcome and the rain a blessing, but a thunderstorm on the great prairie is purely frightening. A body feels small as a roadside flower under the great puffs of clouds. Their soft forms fold over, benign and comforting, until thunder rolls its deep threat. Suddenly the wind tears at you in mighty gusts. The wonder is you are not blown over and rolled to the horizon. Lightning crashes all about. You are helpless. There is no shelter. Faith in God is your only protection.

I had always thought of summer weather as a shawl to lay gently about the shoulders. Now I know it can be a demon weilding vicious whips of wind and lightning. We must be thankful to God for His loving care.

CHAPTER 27

Sod House Tragedy

June, 1865

Dearest Mother and Father,

Our journey to Arizona Territory is a lonely one. I sometimes ruefully wonder, Father, if, on that argument alone, you might have dissuaded us from leaving home three months ago. I truly have no call to complain, for all goes well. Young Virgil is surely happy in this nomadic life. My good husband, Mac, is in fine health, and even the oxen are content. We feel your prayers are with us. I write this note and hope to find a place to post it somewhere in this broad, flat state of Kansas.

Yesterday we saw a wee, distant house. My loneliness made me anxious to stop for a visit with another woman. I think Mac wanted to talk, too. He said he would like to inquire of a local man about the trail. Men are secretive about the things they will admit to.

It was a sod house, typical of the Kansas homes where lumber must be hauled from a great distance. It was plain to see the corn, now 12 inches high, was doing very well in the spot where the sod had been removed to use in building the home and barn. As we drew nearer something seemed amiss.

The man of the place sat on the steps with head bowed in his hands. A little girl, about three, leaned against him; two brothers, a bit older, about Virgil's age or younger, sat on the ground at his feet. It is usual that these children who live far from friends will either hide shyly behind a parent or come joyously to greet a newcomer. The children all looked poorly cared for and could have made use of soap and water, any being available. I noticed the rainbarrel was nearly full.

As we drew up the man stood and lifted his battered old hat in greeting. I have never seen a more haggard or melancholy expression; he looked dazed that we should even be there. Mac jumped from the wagon and offered his hand in greeting. The two rough hands clasped in immediate friendship.

"Is there something I can do for you?" Mac inquired.

"Well,...I...I...We have had such a turrible family tragedy, I guess nothin' can be done right now. I dug the grave whilst the children washed the mud from off their mama and wrapped her in the clean end of the sheet. We're jist pretty well done in after readin' the Bible over her grave."

Then Mac saw the problem and exclaimed, "Why, your roof caved in!" We gazed in anguished astonishment.

"Thet she did," he agreed despondently. He turned his lanky body toward the sod house and shook his head in disbelief. "We had a mighty, tremendous wind and rainstorm day before yistaday then a steady rain for over a day. Never, ever suspected anything was wrong. This mornin' the younguns followed me out to the barn whilst I fed the stock. Maw was not feelin' too well, her bein' in a family way and all. She stayed abed." He paused, swallowed hard and continued. "Looked like the mud-weighted ceilin' boards fell, struck her head and the mud roof buried her." He could say no more. In respect Mac removed his hat, and silently laid a hand on the grieving man's shoulder.

I was already down from the wagon, my arms about the sobbing children. At last they were able to cry, having heard the sad words uttered. Virgil thoughtfully brought a loaf of bread and cut a few slices. The little ones shyly accepted a piece but were able to munch only a bite before handing it back to me, all the while tears made little rivers down their soiled faces.

The oldest child took my hand. I walked along as he led me and all the children out to the grave site. They had placed wild flowers over the freshly dug soil. The older boy explained they would dig some sod to cover the mound and make a nice headstone, too, later on.

I straightened my bonnet to allay my tears and noticed the children all wore well-stitched clothes. I thought how proud their mother must have been of her three little blue-eyed, tow-headed youngsters. My first notice that they lacked a bit of care was only because of the heart-rending job they and their father had just finished. In desperation I retied my apron while my mind searched for diversion.

We plucked some more of the pretty, blue flax blossoms. As we tugged at the tough stems I began to ask the children their names. The oldest boy, Tom, helped the younger ones become less shy. They were Tom, Teddy and 'Tilda. These precious little children really stole my heart, especially chubby 'Tilda. Sturdy Teddy gave her his constant attention and Tom guarded them both.

Virgil heard his Paw call. On our return to the men, Mac reported that we could help Mr. Schmidt the most if we would but stop at the next sod house, just ten miles up the trail, and give his brother's family the news. They would come over to give some help.

We bade them a sad farewell. The little children waved good-bye for so long as we could see them as we drove away to carry the saddest news a stranger could bring.

'Tis a sad note to end on, Mama, but we are well, all three together and send you our love.

In God's care, Molly.

P.S. This evening at bedtime Virgil hugged his fried-egg quilt and with a tear in his eye said softly, "Mama, even my fried-egg quilt could not make me happy if anything ever happened to Papa or you." It has been a sad, thoughtful day. We have much to be thankful for.

CHAPTER 28

Kansas Rest Stop and Wedding Dance

This pale Sabbath dawn does truly rest my soul. Even the wakening bird twitters are more softly sung. It is not often that we can observe this Holy Day as laid down in the commandment. The good Lord knows that there are times when reaching a watering place is more vital than resting on the seventh day. We do not have Moses to strike the rock to provide the life-giving water.

I have been awake at least an hour of this Sabbath so shall lay aside my pen and ink bottle and snuff the candle until later. There is light enough now to read from the Bible. Exodus shall be my choice. Surely the Children of Israel, on their journey to The Promised Land, suffered hardships, trials and tribulations far greater than ours. Virgil is stirring. We can read together until Mac wakens.

I take up my writing this late afternoon. As always, any Sabbath stop-over will have its portion of labor. Several of us ladies finished a washing in the little stream. True, our clothing was muddied during last night's wedding dance. Surely the good Lord looks favorably on an honorable bit of happy pastime. The large caravan that we have traveled apart from had a wedding and of course a dance following. We joined with them for the celebration.

The bend in the river offered a flat, flower-dappled spot for the afternoon ceremony. The young bride's gown was a white dimity with embroidered flowers strewn across the skirt. When she packed that dress I doubt she had any notion it would be worn for such a glorious occasion.

When the minister pronounced them man and wife, the dear little bride became the instant mother of her husband's three sweet little children. Their mother had died over a month ago. The new family is indeed a close and loving group. The new mother will have plenty of help from the family cousins. She will need it, for one of her brood is a wee infant just barely able to sit up.

When the minister's blessing was finished, then began the fiddlers. The dancers whooped it up and stomped about in joyous abandon. The fair flowers were soon tromped to a muddy pulp that spattered our clothes. I'm sure no one noticed. Finally a bonfire lighted the night scene and the hilarity continued until star-lit midnight.

With the half moon rising the travelers soon meandered off to their night's rest for the Sabbath was beginning.

Without a doubt every married couple amongst us was reminded of their own wedding, the vows they made, their own personal resolves and the fun and frolic that finished off the day.

As we three walked to our campsite Mac silently squeezed my arm. A tear of happiness wet my eyes that he should be mindful of my thoughts. Of course he thought it not seemly to make a remark in front of Virgil. For an instant I pressed my head against Mac's shoulder. What a beautiful day it had been.

The wedding party had requested we deny ourselves the frolic and uproarious fun of the wee-hours chivaree. The sudden sounds of clanging pots, pans and wash tubs, horns tooting, even dynamite explosions would be certain to start a cattle stampede. There will be time for chivaree fun when California welcomes the travelers. For tonight knowing that the newlyweds are untying knots from their neatly folded clothes will suffice.

CHAPTER 29

Dust Storm

This morning Virgil said he would like to sleep all day. I asked why as I glanced over to see if he was well. He said he really did not like yesterday's windstorm.

I agreed it would be nice to always sleep away our troubles, then remarked that the slacked wind felt soft today. That cheered him and he decided he would rise and shine, just as though he had a choice.

We do give thanks for our safety and pray for no other such storm, though we know we cannot be coddled. Nature is a part of life here on this earth.

Fortunately my carefully wrapped journal fared well. No invading blasts of sand reached into its covers and of course the tightly stoppered ink bottle remained closed. More importantly, our wagon's cover withstood the blast.

Yesterday's sky began pleasantly but fresh winds strengthened by mid morning. Then a yellow haze appeared overhead. At noon Virgil noticed the clouds were pink on the lower side. We became gradually aware that a dust storm brewed in our direction.

By mid afternoon our wagon frequently shuddered from strong gusts. Mac thought it best to stop. The wind was not directly in our faces but we all suffered from breathing the dust-laden air that also irritated our eyes.

Fortunately we came to a swail and entered a small grove of cottonwoods that gave us shelter. We kept to the edge of the trees lest some of their great limbs fall on us. The oxen were tethered to the north side of the wagon for what protection it offered them.

As always in the presence of trees, Virgil began gathering firewood that he found about us. He collected a few handfulls before the wind's intensity increased, until the child was forced to take cover. This time he could not sit under the wagon as he does in a rain shower. He needed to be out of the fierce, stinging wind to avoid being blown about like a tumble weed.

Mac worked at bracing the buffeted wagon with the extra planks that are always carried alongside. What useful items they have proved to be. To the hoops of our wagon he tied ropes that were then snugged around nearby trees. Between the two nearest trees I helped stretch a length of canvas as a wind-break. Controlling that canvas proved the most difficult thing I ever tried to do. In order to hold it, I wrapped an end around my wrist and arm. Before Mac had time to secure the other three corners I thought the wind would tear my arm off, but I braced myself with the help of a tree. With great effort we finished the job. We climbed inside our wagon fortress as a blast of sand caught us. From inside the wagon I happened to turn in time to give a mighty tug to Mac's arm. He stumbled in besides me.

"Water," he gasped. "Wet towels for our faces." As I grabbed for the towels I saw the trees outside disappear, obliterated from view by a flying wall of dirt, sand, and pebbles. Tying shut the opening fly rebuffed the invading grit only a little. Wet towels to our faces, we sank down to the wagon bed.

I silently prayed we would not blow over and that the oxen would not suffocate. Mac had placed masks over their faces.

Some long minutes later the roar of the wind subsided. The grit, still striking our wagon, sounded like a sleet storm. We dared not venture out for fear of another blast of wind. Gradually the pelting lessened and the light grew brighter outside.

Mac hurried immediately to the tethered oxen. He stayed to calm them with petting and brushing of their gritty hides. How grateful we were that they were both all right and our wagon had withstood the brunt of the storm.

It was early but I set about laying out supper. For a certainty I planned no fire for cooking. Cold cornbread with a bit of jelly, cold fried bacon left from breakfast, and the usual tepid water all tasted good but well sprinkled with sandstorm grit. To bite or chew our food proved so unpleasant we broke off small bits and washed our supper down whole.

Virgil was uncommonly quiet at supper as though he had to concentrate to eat in this strange way. For once I did not have to say, "Eat, now. Let your vittals stop your mouth." I'd have rather had him talking.

The storm abated until we could easily see way past the wagon tongue. Though protected inside we found sparse comfort with grit down our necks, in our sleeves and in our shoes. Mac told squirming Virgil he could consider this scouring from the sand his Saturday night's bath. Virgil grinned good naturedly saying he would prefer the bath this time.

In preparing our covers for the night, we slowly and carefully poured off the grit and pebbles that had blown into the wagon and into the blanket folds. Our clothing we shook out as best we could. Careful though we were, we slept in gravel, cramped in the wagon, but grateful for protection. Tomorrow, after cleaning out the wagon we will all have fresh clothing.

CHAPTER 30

Vanity

I looked in the mirror today. I am sorry I had time to do so. It is a mistake to show such vanity on the trail. I found I am almost brown as an Indian. Mother would cry if she could see me now. I know she would. Ah, my poor mother. Always she had been unseemly proud of my fair English skin.

A sunbonnet covered my head to shield my complexion at any time I was out-of-doors. On the trail I have, from habit, never failed to take the same precaution. I could see my hands were brown as last years berries. Now my face is a perfect match. So who cares? I am past caring if Mother is not to see me.

'Twas but a foolish notion that I used the mirror to see how dusty my hair has become. It has not been washed since our stop at the Chariton River in Missouri. That was a lovely spot with a little waterfall made by a fallen log across the clear stream.

It is not likely we will find such a spot again for we have few streams and fewer trees. I have soft soap ready in any event. To wash this dust from my brown hair that now looks almost grey, would be a true joy. Certainly cleanliness is not a vanity.

CHAPTER 31

New Mexico Territory

After the green of spring in Missouri and the tall grass of Kansas Territory we have a sparse dull green in New Mexico Territory. I try not to think of the comparison. The mornings are blessedly cool. We start out by first light. Virgil says the sun will not find us for a while. When it does I begin to feel its penetration to my bones. I feel its heat all through my body like a hot drink on a cold day. Each breath pours in more heat. I restrain myself from even a worried sigh. I do not complain. Mac has burden enough without our wails. Virgil is understanding and is easily guided to silence or distraction. Once I breathed a prayer of thanks for a breeze that had sprung up. Mac suggested best we pray the breeze did not become a wind that would whip the sand about us until we were unable to see. That I remember well.

There are distant rock cliffs surrounding us. The great space between seems a land neglected by even God. What had been sparse grass is dead, yellow, crunching and brown, crackling underfoot. A few short stubbles of weedy bushes are seen in occasional clumps. There are low woody plants with only dead branches and leaves so few there is little that is fit for the oxen. The branches seem a likely use for supper's fire. It is with only the greatest struggle that Virgil can break them off. They are of no use to the plant and resist being of use to us, too.

If rocks were food we would have more than plenty, and the strangest kind. They are unbelievable. In a place off to the left of our path, the land sloped gently down from all directions to form a basin as if it had at one time held a great lake. Through this dished valley are strange purple-brown rock mounds looking like monstrous loaves of bread, badly burned and left here a long, long way from the oven.

There are other mounds of rock that are layered, flat topped, and standing alone thoughout the desert. Some have a white rock topping like an iced cake. The topping is falling away in great slabs. "Mama," Virgil said, "the mounds are the giants tables. The mother giant told the family not to lean their elbows on the table. They did it anyway and broke off the table edges." A good explanation, and perhaps Virgil is learning about elbows on the table. It has been months since we have had a table to lean our elbows on.

Next Day

Today the rock mounds are in layered colors. Some mounds are colored identically to their surrounding neighbors. Farther away many have a purple cast. Some are completely without color and show only a dead gray. Sometimes a greenish gray appears that looks positively poisonous. At first I was cheered by the thought we will not be living here. Then I realized the farther we have journeyed the more desolate our surroundings have become. Will it be better in Arizona Territory? I pray it won't worsen. Truly I doubt it could.

Next Day
Our Rocky Diversions

Today the distant cliff sides look like giant people, Virgil says. Their pointed heads looking far away are not looking down at us. No telling what they are thinking. The remainder of the cliff toward the base is made of wide bands and thinner layers of pink and red rock. Farther on, another cliff side has no color, only wide bands of dirty white. This evening the near cliff sides were bright pink from an afternoon shower that cooled the air, but sadly no rain fell on us.

Great arched portals appear carved into their walls. There is no opening. They seem closed or unfinished. A few of the portals have an open cave. Some are so large and deep Mac says the Indians lived there. We saw no signs of anyone. Virgil says he would like to live in such a cave. I think I am dreaming.

Mac says nothing of the strange scenery. He secretly worries whether the wagon rims will wear through on this rough, rocky trail or fall from the dried-out wagon wheels. He worries over the oxen. He was petting Joe and rubbing his ears; he asked Joe if he wanted more water and Pete if he was hungry. For ourselves we have food supply in plenty. It is the oxen, the wagon wheels, the rims and the water that concern Mac.

He shot an antelope this evening. That renewed our hope. All will be well. Game is not plentiful but it is here. Surely we will find water that will renew our supply when we cross the Rio Grande later on.

CHAPTER 32

Wagon Mound and Ft. Union

Our journey drags slowly on. Wearisome it is, yet we say our thanks for each morning given us and wonder what is ahead for the new day. According to Mac's little drawing of the country, we will come to a rock called Wagon Mound. We reach it several days before we see the river valley of the Rio Grande.

Just having a special landmark to look for somehow makes the journey less tedious. Virgil said he would spy the mound before I did. We did not know it would appear slowly against the brilliant, blue horizon. First a wee hump grew against the sky, then with each step of the oxen the lump increased slowly as a leaf unfurling.

Finally Virgil pointed ahead and explained to me that there was a lump up ahead but that it was many miles away and much too small to be a wagon-sized rock. After the noon rest he readily agreed the rock was getting much bigger; it could possibly be a wagon-sized rock. Before mid-afternoon the great Wagon Mound stood against the sky, a monstrous outcropping of rock that looked very much like our own, tiny covered wagon. Virgil did not think he could declare himself as the "I spy" winner because the shape did not suddenly appear.

Not very far away, but farther than we would have cared to walk, there stood two similar mounds. The smaller one Virgil named Bread Loaf. The larger one covered much more area than Wagon Mound but did not stand as high. Virgil says this one is Haystack, where the Indians feed their horses. You could even see where they had been eating.

Virgil's lively imagination at work on the scene had helped us pass another day on our way to Fort Union.

Everyone here at Fort Union is in a festive mood. They had a birthday celebration followed by a dance. We would have enjoyed being here for that. We are camped inside the fort grounds and feel quite safe. No Indian problems have occurred for some time.

Mac is busy. He has made arrangements for the oxen to be shod, new rims put on the wheels, dickered for new oak axles, and, of all things, has arranged for the washing to be done up. Land sakes, I don't know when I have been such a lady!

Virgil is overjoyed to have children to play with. Mac has given him free reign as long as he stays within the stockade and keeps out of the streets. There is a great deal of traffic here. Mule trains, yokes of oxen and cavalry horses are constantly moving about or in and out of the fort. Also Virgil must stay away from the well-stocked merchandise store or commissary. Mac said I should see if I need anything from it.

I declare, it is scarcely seemly for me to be out and about among all these men without my husband. Perhaps the soldiers are more accustomed to seeing women going about their business. I think I will try the store tomorrow. Mac says we will not leave for several days.

A day later…

I went to the commissary with a young woman named Catherine Smith. She and her family are traveling from Missouri to Santa Fe. Her three older children were off playing and minding their three-year-old sister. Catherine carried the baby who is not quite walking. She said she hopes he would be running about within the next three months. I knew she meant her seventh babe will be born by then. Land sakes! She must be a good manager with six children to do for. Her two-year-old that I held by the hand was a well-behaved lad.

We must have looked bug-eyed walking about the store. It has been a long time since I've seen so many goods laid out to buy. I thought the strangest thing was green shoe thread. Who would be mending their black shoes with green thread? Catherine bought a few yards of diaper cloth. She said the old diapers would be made into union suits for the little boys. She stitches them up whilst they travel but the buttonholes she does by the fire-light. The moving wagon is too jiggly for such fine work. What a good manager!

I bought handsome red and green suspenders for both Mac and Virgil. Catherine urged me to get something for myself saying, "If you don't get something for your own self you just might never get a thing." I agreed with her though I know it is not so with me and generous Mac. I did long to buy a pair of white cotton stockings, but thought better of it. I know my skirt will never rise above my shoetops. However, I imagined if it should, there I would be in white cotton stockings. No, I'd best stay with the black and so bought a pair. It will be nice to have some that are not mended. I bought some darning thread, too, and a new darning needle. I don't know who borrowed the one I brought from home. I must take better care.

Leaving Fort Union I saw what I missed coming in. The constant heavy traffic coming and going in and out of the Fort has gouged axle-deep ruts in the fine dry soil. No one ever becomes stuck. The animals' hooves seem to pack it all down again as long as it does not rain. I might add it seldom does that.

CHAPTER 33

Santa Fe

We are ready to leave Santa Fe, and I am reluctant to go. The city was a great disappointment to me on arrival, and I spent as little time on its dusty streets as possible. Mac was extra thoughtful in purchases just for me in an effort to cheer me a bit. Spending time at the water's edge, washing and cooking beneath the great shady cottonwood trees cheered me the most. I feel revived and rested. Having a group of ladies I could neighbor with is the reason for my cheerfulness.

The wagon is in fine shape with new tires on the wheels and two springs replaced. Food barrels have been replenished and water barrels are splashing full. We are leaving this noon to get a bit on down the road before nightfall.

Now it comes at me full force. The road. The treeless, dusty road that glares back and burns the eyes; the breeze that does not cool but parches mouth and throat while fine sand is sifted between my teeth. But we are nearing journey's end. Arizona Territory and Santa Fe are not as far apart as Santa Fe and Lima, Ohio where we departed five months ago on March first.

I do believe Mac would have come all this great distance just to put his gear in good condition again. He itemized everything we have worn thin or worn completely through and replaced it. He has replaced all apparel. Fort Union did not have all the goods Mac felt were needed. I think Santa Fe is the jumping off place of this world as the Canary Islands were for Columbus' sailors in his day. I continue to worry more and more about our journey, but I say naught of it.

I do not admonish Mac for his spending. He has surely gotten us through all these months by his good planning regardless of my silent fretting. Mac has even replaced the oxen. Virgil was in tears to say good-bye to the old friends. They have taken us faithfully through many rough spots and even saved us from miring in the Missouri mud.

Mac explained we have some high climbing to make yet and pointed out that the great Raton Pass before Ft. Union was very tiring for our oxen. We are to replace them with a younger yoke that is well broken in, and, I might add, one that has been better fed and watered these past months.

While in Santa Fe I would not stay in the city amidst the general rubble, noisy travelers, shouting wagoneers, scrawny dogs slinking about, and unwashed children. It would have been Virgil's favorite place to be, but I was taking no chances of losing track of the child again.

Mac deposited us on the banks of the river with several families. Some of the younguns went fishing upstream where it wasn't deep enough to drown a tadpole while the women and I were glad to find a place to wash our clothes. The river was low, but we found deep pools that we used to good advantage.

It distressed me that I was so improperly dressed in my new clothes for scrubbing wash on the rocks. Finally I became accustomed to it, but it served to hurry me to finish sewing the new calico dress to allow the change to more ordinary clothing. I declare, to have three clean dresses at one time seems mighty high toned.

Strangely enough we must travel north now in order to get between the mountains and find the pass to take us south into Arizona Territory. Traveling in New Mexico Territory we find long merchant trains on their way to Mexico for trading. They have deeply rutted the roads, as was true at Fort Union. Our oxen strain and Mac patiently guides them to keep astride the axle-deep cuts.

Out of the ruts and onto dry ground the rough pathway presents a problem of another kind. The wheels are seldom on the same level. A rear wheel will be rolling over a rocky point and the opposite front wheel will drop into a low spot until the wracked wagon looks ready to break apart. For the day long it continues. Ruts or rocks, Virgil and I generally walk if we have the shade of the wagon to protect us. Mac still rides some of the time to see the wretched path ahead and to better guide the oxen; only when the way is smooth can he have the relief of walking. Surely Arizona Territory will be an improvement. How could it possibly worsen?

One cheering thought—though the summer rains left the roads mightily rutted, the grass has responded in luxuriant growth. I truly am amazed, for I was convinced nothing would grow in this strange world.

CHAPTER 34

Bone Thin

As we leave the shady river banks of a stream at Santa Fe, we have more than another month of scorching travel before reaching Arizona Territory. I pray there be shade at our journey's end.

Mac says we must be on a sharper lookout for Indians. There are more here-a-bouts than in Kansas, some friendlier than others. Right off Virgil wanted to know why they were not friendly.

"Oh, they might be riled because we are crossing their hunting grounds. Best we keep a sharp eye out and be prepared not to act frightened.

"Virgil, if I tell you to get into the wagon, you do just that, cover up and keep quiet, no matter about bravery. Molly, if you have to shoot be certain to hold the gun tight against your shoulder and you won't get knocked off the seat. Just have the gun handy-by; there may be no need to shoot.

"They'll want food, more than likely. A loaf of bread and a squash will be enough. If there's a passel of them they can have those old clothes we just shucked out of.

"If they are wearing war paint and riding around ornery-like, then the show of our guns may be all that's necessary to make them vamoose."

"But Paw, why do I have to keep covered?"

"Well, I don't want them to think they could carry off a nice little yeller-haired child. They aren't likely to carry off what they cannot see."

I said both Virgil and I had best ride inside no matter if the rough road shook our bones.

"Paw, what if they shoot our oxen?" Virgil asked what I did not want to think about.

"I reckon we'd take shanks mare back to Santa Fe."

Yes, I thought, if we are alive and able to walk. The day wore on to evening. We had exhausted ourselves keeping that sharp lookout. I longed for darkness when Indians seldom attack.

Suddenly Virgil pointed across to the desert horizon. "What is that hump of a thing out there?"

Mac thought it surely looked like a horse and rider. We silently watched it approach, each with our own fears. When Mac reminded us to keep watch in other directions, too, our fears increased with the sudden thought that we might have been tricked by a lone horse while a hoard of rascals crept upon us from our blind side. We kept a more sweeping watch.

As the horse shape grew closer we could make out a rider slumped over the horse's neck and barely able to stay astride. He was dressed like an Indian and bone thin.

Mac drove the wagon to cross their trail. The horse could barely stay on his feet. It stopped as Mac swung to the ground, lifted the young rider down, and laid him in our wagon.

I brought water to the exhausted traveler. Mac kept the watch and Virgil led the horse to the shade of the wagon where he gave the animal sips of water from his hand. Softly crooning, he sponged the pony's dusty, brown and white hide with cooling water.

My new patient with burned, brown skin, wearing a breachcloth and bear claw necklace was not an Indian child. His hair was too fair. As I wiped his face and arms with a wet cloth, he slowly came to consciousness. Finally a sip of water slipped between his lips. He could swallow at last. Giving sips of water was all we could do until he revived a bit more.

Toward dark we three ate bread for our supper and Virgil fell asleep early. The cool night air helped return normal temperature to the wanderers and we stopped sponging them down.

Food was their next need. Mac soaked bread in water for the horse. My patient slowly swallowed a softened slice, bit by bit. Sleep, water, and food we gave slowly the night long.

At dawn's first light sleepy Virgil was roused to keep watch while Mac and I slept for an hour or so. On wakening we found Virgil sitting alertly, gun across his lap; our brave guardian. The fried-egg quilt covered the new friend.

I lighted a fire, fried meat grease for biscuits and boiled up some cornmeal mush. The smell of food wakened our new family member. Virgil offered him a spoon and a bowl of mush. He held the spoon and slowly drank the mush, watching us intently. Mac joined us to announce the horse had lived through the night. The boy showed no interest. Mac faced him, pointed to himself and spoke slowly, "Mac." Then pointing to our bewildered friend asked, "What is your name?" There was no response at first. The family was introduced as Mac, smiling, repeated the lesson. The child brightened with understanding and pointing to himself said, "Small Boy."

Mac, using signs and words, told Small Boy we could take him back to Santa Fe. Small Boy nodded and repeated, "Santa Fe."

"He has been with the Indians a long time, but we might find out where he belongs," Mac said as we loaded our gear for an early start.

Mac and I began the sweeping watch while the two boys sat in the wagon and began making conversation, using sign language and teaching each other words. Small Boy even began to smile and laugh.

In spite of the many stops to water the horse we reached Santa Fe before sundown. At the oldest inn on the square Mac began to make inquires. No one knew of a lost child until a fourteen-year-old lad heard the tale. He said he had a lost brother, stolen by the Indians at least four years ago. His parents had searched eastward-traveling wagon trains but never found their son who was only five when he disappeared.

The young lad, Evan, went to fetch his parents while we brought Small Boy into the tavern. Clothing too large and tattered did not prevent the weeping parents from recognizing their long-lost child. Such rejoicing I have never seen. Though Small Boy's name was really Joseph, he was known as Joe, The Miracle Child.

Joe had been stolen at age five and given to a grieving Indian Mother whose baby had died. When his foster Mother died Joseph tried to make his way back to his own family. He had only an idea of the direction to Santa Fe and no idea of the distance. He and his sturdy pony had traveled for four or five days. He was indeed a Miracle Child.

Before we left at dawn the following day, Virgil came to me and quietly said he wanted Joe to have the fried-egg quilt. I agreed it would be a nice remembrance gift. My thought was, though colorful, the quilt's fragile condition was pronounced, and just the thing to be exchanged by two little boys.

CHAPTER 35

Language

Virgil had been somber since we departed from Joseph. I believe he hoped the child would become our adopted son. Of course, he is proud that he played a part in returning the long-lost child to his family.

On the way out of Santa Fe we passed our old campground where the children had such fun laughing, splashing and ducking until they were tuckered out. Their only chores were to gather firewood and carry water; the only restriction—stay close to camp. I am certain Virgil understands that restraint even better now.

It was an idyllic spot. Virgil wanted to stay forever. Like Virgil, I was loath to leave friends, but also glad to go and get on with the journey and be done with it.

It is hard to think what Arizona Territory will be like. I ope not like Santa Fe with its rush and hustle yet a dreary, dusty place. Arizona Territory is bound to have likeable people and most likely there will be a child or two Virgil can cotton to.

This afternoon as we walked Virgil broke his long silence asking, "Maw, why do people sound so different when they talk?"

I was taken aback with such a question and inquired what he meant.

"Well," he sighed, "at the river there was one batch of younguns from Atlanta and they never said things the way I do and not even like the other boys, either."

"Did you notice if they talked like their Maw?"

"Yes, I think they did, Mama. They all sounded alike. It was a little funny sometimes but I tried not to laugh."

"If they talked like their parents that is what you would expect. Children learn to talk like their parents."

"But why is it different, Mama?"

"Their parents or grandparents lived in different countries of Europe. When they came across the Atlantic Ocean to our country they talked the language of their homeland and began to talk our English, too. And so it sounds different. You remember how your granny talked a bit of Scottish with her English, don't you?"

"Yes, I do remember Granny. She would laugh and say, 'Hoot, Mahn! Gee a lang wi' ye!' I wish I talked in a different way, too."

"Perhaps you do to some of your friends," I pointed out.

Virgil looked up at me and grinned.

CHAPTER 36

The Rio Grande and the Sign

It has been a long pull up out of the Rio Grande Valley. The oxen needed many little rests over and above the hourly stop. At times it has seemed intolerable to stand by for that wait in the oppressive heat, but we must be very careful not to overtire the beasts.

Now that we have left the luxuriant cottonwoods by the river we find no shade except inside the wagon or sometimes walking in the wagon's shadow. Virgil finds the glaring sand and rock too hot for bare feet. We walk in the cool early mornings. They seem to reassure us that the day cannot repeat yesterday's heated torture. We are grateful for the cool nights and travel by moonlight when we can.

As the oxen pulled us up from the valley this morning, below us the fog lay in all the depressions like a miracle of lakes beckoning us to stop and fill our water barrels. We know better than to waste our time, but it was a thing of beauty to be thankful for.

Time is becoming more important out here where we are surrounded by nothing, nothing but rocks. Our food supply is in sufficient quantity to keep body and soul together. The oxen find some good in this standing dry grass. The overpowering worry is the water supply. We have left the river with all we could carry. Will we have enough to supply our needs before finding water again? I say naught of it for I would not have my fears weighing on Mac. I see little evidence that this strange place will yield moisture. Mac says this is the dry season, so there must be a wet season, too, and this dry grass had a chance to grow then. I am astonished that this strange rocky land can produce anything worthwhile. Besides providing standing hay for the oxen the grass does make a fair fire if twisted tightly and wrapped with another wisp. It is enough to bring the buffalo chips to burning. We are careful to keep our fire in the sunken-earth fire pot well contained. A prairie fire is a terrible thing.

We see no animals now save for a scurrying lizard now and then. Virgil has long since stopped trying to catch one of them. This strange scenery is our daily diversion. It is ever changing and nothing like anything we've seen before. The distant steep ridges of rock are flat on top but built up of layers of different colors of pink. Then again there will be a gray-green color that seems to be a vile, unrelenting threat. To what, I do not know, and so it is more evil. At times I must remind myself that God's hand has formed heaven and earth lest I find myself wondering if Beelzebub had a hand in forming this menacing land.

Some walls of rock are not level but tipped up like a table and driven into the earth as if by some great force. Now and again across the distant plain there will appear great conical lumps. Many of them have a sinister gray at their base or the complete hillock is gray. Virgil says they are ant hills as big as a house. We must wend our way among the ant hills and find a pass that will lead us through the level distant ridges. I must remember these level ridges are called mesas.

At evening today, against the sky on a high mesa, we saw an Indian village. Then a miracle met our eyes. There, raised up before us in a waning light, rose the white steeple of a church. A sign of Christianity in this desolate land. I felt God had given us a token of His blessing and lifted it up before us. I bowed my head in shame and asked forgiveness for thinking this might be the land of the devil.

Mac said because of the heat we could not give the oxen the added burden of climbing up to the village summit to the church and the cross. He was right, of course, so I did not let myself be disappointed. I resolutely kept in my mind's eye the beauty of that spire in the sky.

CHAPTER 37

Dead River and Petrified Forest

When we crossed Dead River such a name did not surprise me, not at all. Most things are dead out here on this desert. The wonder is that anything ever lived. Many of the little hills we pass are that deathly grey color. No plants grow on them.

Today we had a huge, black shower cloud off to the north of us. Grateful we are for even a distant rain that cools the air. I did not think we would be wet by the storm but it blew over us. Torrents of rain fell. It was wonderful. We drew up to a stop in the lee of a grey hill for what protection it afforded.

Of course the wash basin and bucket were positioned to catch what water they could. For such a hard shower we caught little. The rivulets surprised us. The rain began immediately running in active little rills that joined to make larger ones and finally a fair-sized stream was flowing below us.

Muddy it was and useless. None of it seemed to soak down into the sand as it passed along. We were up high enough that we could look back and catch a glimpse of where Dead River had been a sandy bed. Imagine our surprise to see it was no longer dead. Indeed, it was a raging river rolling sizeable boulders along in its path. It would have been total disaster to have been driving in the dry river bed. Any wilting plant parched for a drop of rain would have been torn out, roots and all, in the path of such action.

Virgil had fun squishing his toes in the rivulets though he did say it was not as soft as Missouri mud. The ground is covered with coarse sharp gravel that is glass-like.

When the sun came shining down on us we were in for another surprise. The whole countryside had taken on a new coloring. The rocks, the grey hills and the distant pink and red cliffs were bright and shining as though a light had been turned on inside them. This unexpected beauty surrounded us, while we breathed in the cool, rain-washed air. For the first time the desert had become a glorious gem.

Virgil coaxed me to step down from the wagon to feel the side of a hill. I knew from its appearance it would be rough and gritty but I lighted from the wagon to please him. To my astonishment I learned that the grey hill had become a mass of slippery clay. It is no surprise that nothing grows on them. I like them even less simce they are slimey. We used the dirty rain caught in the basin to rinse off Virgil's feet.

Mac explained, "The wind whips the sand into the air; the rain washes the sand back down and we have sandy rain."

We emptied the bucket-catch carefully so as to let the sand settle out. The oxen were grateful for their little sip. We had a few hours of travel yet before making camp in the newly washed, cooled air. It gave us a feeling of being transplanted to an astonishing new world.

Another amazing sight met our eyes today. Great logs lay here and there on the ground. To begin with I could not understand how they ever grew to be such tall trees in this desert. They were broken in huge round chunks and lay there as though the tree had been cut through in many places with a saw and were ready for loading on a wagon. Very few of the chunks were broken open. On closer inspection we found them to be great heavy colorful rocks that we could not budge. Such colors as you have never seen. Imagine seeing purple, dark red, orange, white, grey, brown, green, grey-blue, and black all mixed together. Never would you see such colors in a piece of a tree or even a rock.

Mac let us wander about in amazement for a spell then he told us these were petrified trees that grew a long, long time ago and had turned to stone. It truly was more than is possible to believe, but there they were, trees that did not rot but turned to stone. Virgil remarked, "I wonder what I'll dream about tonight."

CHAPTER 38

Tribulations

Tribulations! Oh, the tribulations we have endured! We have suffered enough dear Lord! But it is not just to blame the Lord. We came of our own free will and of our own decision. But we have suffered; how we have suffered!

We have walked and ridden in freezing cold, been snow-bound, crossed roaring treacherous rivers, faced poisonous vipers, feared burning up in a prairie fire, and nearly suffocated in a wind storm. Yes, we had the balm of a green oasis, a precious respite, before crossing this arid wilderness, this desolate land of unrelenting heat, with water rationed in pitiful amounts that never slake the thirst of man or beast. Now we pass these endless white cliffs with soil that clearly is but a wasteland.

Since leaving the great expanse of prairie grasses I have been ill with the thought our destination will be but a barren land where we cannot grow a thing we can live on. It is too late to turn back. Could we have done so, I would long ago have persuaded Mac to turn East. It is too late now. No, this venture can do nothing but end in disaster of some fiendish sort.

Now to our plight another tribulation is added. Before us there is an arroyo that is too deep to be crossed. We cannot drive down into it. We could not drive out the far side if we could drive in from this side. We simply cannot cross.

Nowhere are there trees that could afford us material for a simple bridge. Mac has walked five miles farther upstream seeking a better crossing. Virgil and I have walked in the opposite direction. The chasm grew deeper. There is no hope. None. We cannot dig the banks down to allow our passage. This arroyo is gouged out of layer upon layer of solid rock.

Discouraged, we have eaten a cold supper. Night descends. We will not sleep for this dilemma, this rock, is our pillow.

CHAPTER 39

Solution

My dear father always said when the Lord sends a problem He also sends a solution if we but look for it. Last night I dreamed Mac was smiling and this morning he was smiling. He had the solution to our dilemma, and put all of us, grown-ups, child and beasts to work. I am so weary I can scarce hold the pen to write.

When Mac walked upstream yesterday in search of a lower bank for crossing, he found a spot where there is a heap of stones scattered along in the arroyo bottom. Before he went to sleep last night he thought he had the answer to our dilemma. He would pile, indeed, we all would pile rocks until we filled the arroyo from bank to bank. This done we could cross on a bridge. He is certain that is why the rocks are there. Someone had built a crossing years ago but a flood had washed it out. Now it is for us to rebuild, and thankful we are for the rocks. Mac thinks he has a plan that will keep the rock bridge in use for a good long spell.

First off this morning we drove to the rock spot, as Virgil calls it, and set up camp. I will like staying in one place for a while. How pleasant it would be if only we had a tree or two for shade. What a spoiled notion! There will be no time for lolling about. We will be here only a week or two or however long this bridge building takes.

Mac laid down some rules for us all to obey. Do not work until we are too tired. Rest will be important. A worker who is tired may have accidents.

Another thing that is important to remember is what might be living among the rocks.

"Like snakes?" suggested Virgil, nodding wisely.

"Oh, yes, and baby snakes will not be friendly, either. We are disturbing the home of other critters, too, that bite, sting and are downright unfriendly, so we must look out for them and us. So always wear shoes and gloves and always turn over a rock before you pick it up to see what you may be disturbing. A scorpion, spider, snake or thousand legger might be quietly waiting for a bite of something, especially like a boy from Ohio. So remember, rest, wear shoes and gloves, look carefully at a rock on both sides before you pick it up."

Virgil laughed and nodded but earnestly assured his Paw he would be careful of the three rules. They are all hard rules to follow but we will work together on them. The hardest is the one about resting before we get too tired.

CHAPTER 40

The Bridge and the Sore Toe

Mac plans to keep the stone bridge from washing away when it rains. The water will pass under the bridge through two triangular tunnels of flat rock. Another flat rock, placed across the apex of each tunnel, will have the weight of the bridge bearing down on it holding all in place like an archway. This seems a likely plan, but it means finding some large flat rocks for the tunnel walls. The sides of the arroyo are layer upon layer of flat rocks. All we must do is remove pieces of the layers. Simple! A simple task, indeed!

Mac worked at this while Virgil and I carried rock to fill around and over the tunnels. Always we looked for any varmint before picking up the burden, and burden it soon became. Mac warned us to go easy until our muscles were used to the work. The problem was to know ahead of time that we had done too much. Aching exhaustion always told us when to rest.

It helped to stop and do different kinds of work, too. When Mac was splitting out the layers he needed, we could hold the bar while he pounded it to split the rock free. Then two heavy iron hooks were positioned to haul the rock out. An oxen, down in the arroyo, worked the rock loose with the hooks as we guided the beast back and forth, back and forth. The rock edged out like a loose tooth, Virgil said. This mining of the layered rocks lowered the height of the banks, perhaps by a foot. Only eight feet remained to fill with rocks!

It was all incredibly hard work. The day long there was no shade except in or under the wagon. Nary a cloud passed by to give relief. We tied rags about our foreheads to keep streams of perspiration from stinging our eyes. Another cloth around the neck helped us feel cool. We learned to rest much of the mid-day. This became the time I prepared our food. By evening I was too weary to fuss about a meal.

The oxen got little protection until the sun was low enough to cast a wagon shadow. By that time we were back at the rock work. Only one beast was in use at a time. We spelled them off, allowing them time to chew their cud. It seemed too bad they could not understand and rejoice in the progress made. They went doggedly, placidly about their work, heads nodding in rhythm with their feet, snatching a morsel of grass or a weed to chew on now and again. Mac gave them frequent cups of water, being careful they spilled not a drop. We three workers went frequently to the drinking bucket, too. We are now accustomed to tepid water, complain little, and are happy we have something to drink. For a special treat I hang a cloth-wrapped jar of water in the wagon's shade. Above it hangs a punctured water can which drips on the jar's cover. The water evaporates from the cloth, which cools the jar of water, and we have a refreshing drink. It wastes none of the drip. It is useful for washing when caught in the basin. Long ago we used all the vinegar and ginger to flavor our drinks.

In three days we carried a goodly pile of rocks, all from the bottom of the arroyo where someone's first bridge washed away in a heavy storm. Our first tunnel looks beautiful and takes up a lot of space that we rock carriers will not have to fill. In three of four more days we hope to have carried several more feet of rock to be piled around the second tunnel. When it is finished Mac will be able to help us carry rocks.

From the stems of scraggly bushes and some heavy leather Mac fashioned a triangular sled. On this we pulled several rocks at one time. It was a helpful carrier and we wore out three of them. Bending low to pull it we suffered the agony of backache, but it was better than the long carry of heavy rocks to the bridge. Virgil said we were the Israelites hauling rocks for the Egyptians. I said it was good we did not have to cut and fit the rocks. We heaved them into place and rolled them about until they fitted snuggly, then chinked smaller pieces about them.

The bridge is nine feet wide at the bottom. At the top a rope line will guide us to keep the width at seven feet. Virgil wonders if we will ever get that wide. Mac directed us to fit the rocks to slant in a bit toward the center, as Virgil said, like stacking a woodpile.

It is not like wood to my mind. Wood is not so heavy and these rocks are astonishingly beautiful. I pointed out to Virgil the patterns of moss and three different colors of lichens growing. He said, "Mama, how did God have time to make the rocks pretty, too?" I suggested perhaps he had put the sun to work on this job because the rocks underneath the pile had not grown any decorations at all.

We have run low on water. Both man and beast have consumed more than usual in our heavy work. During our rest periods Mac made a leather carrier to fit over the oxen's back. It will carry a small keg of water on either side. With this he plans to walk back to a spring by the white-barked sycamores, fill up with water, and return in a day and a half. He can make the trip more quickly that way than hauling the wagon up and down those hills. Virgil and I will stay at camp and heave some more rocks in place. The bridge is almost high enough to cross. Perhaps two feet more can be added by the time Mac returns. If we do there will be no time for tiddlywinks. With a week or two of water supply, we can finish the crossing and get on with our journey, which I long to finish. We are fortunate water is close by and the delay will be short.

Mac is making use of the waning light to go for more water. I will close my ink bottle and work with Virgil. He is calling me urgently now.

An urgent call it was, too. Poor boy! He accidentally rolled a heavy rock on his left great toe. No more rock work tonight.

CHAPTER 41

Water Trip

By mid afternoon Virgil's toe had ceased throbbing, especially when he did not try to hop about. He was quite pleased to see that it was turning black, and carefully used the water drip plan to keep it cool but nary a tear did he shed. I told him that we should have a ceremony and present him with a badge for courage and hard work when his Paw came home. That pleased him but he gallantly offered me a badge also. I laughed and assured him that my toes were all in good shape.

Since we had filled in enough rocks I turned my attention to getting a start on supper plans. I was slicing away at our small supply of bacon when I noticed the ox, Beasty, begin to stir from his placid cud chewing. First the ears pointed then the head swung about toward the east with keen attention. I was surprised when he began a soft lowing, something I have never heard from Beasty. I had no other cause to have worry but wondered if this might be his alarm signal. Soon I heard sounds approaching from the east.

It seemed too early for Mac and I wondered if I should prepare for a visitor of some sort. As I watched I caught a glimpse of Mac's hat coming over the rise. At once I knew relief. Until then I had no qualms of being alone with Virgil. Little had I thought of what might have been.

Mac expressed unusual pleasure in being back and hugged us soundly I thought.

I was the only one who noticed how Joe and Beasty responded to being together again, rubbing heads and noses. Mac gave proper attention to Virgil's injured toe, but it did seem a trifle short. The ceremony will be held later.

The bridge was inspected and approved with real enthusiasm. It was ready for use. Yes, it was not as high as he had planned but it would do very well when we used the famous platform boards as a top dressing for the wheels to run on.

I began to get the feeling that Mac was in a hurry to get off right now. I enquired if we should have a fire for preparing supper. His short answer of no was repeated as though I should know better than to ask.

There were not a great many things to load on or in the wagon. I attended to that chore. Virgil sat morosely, sad at leaving this spot of hardest labor he had ever had. I did not mention that the water barrels were only half filled, knowing the explanation would come soon enough.

When the oxen were yoked we were ready to take off in less than an hour after Mac's arrival. Virgil and I watched Mac line up the team for a straight approach to our wonderful bridge over the arroyo. He walked the oxen over their path of planks, while we two watched the wheels roll smoothly along just as they should. The rocks crunched down a bit and Mac held his breath as Virgil and I did. Everything was perfect! "Hurrah!" shouted Virgil, then climbed into the front seat to hold the reins while Mac and I, grinning at our great success, loaded the wonderful planks into their place alongside the load.

I wanted to shout, "Hallelujah," or have at least a short ceremony, but I could see it would have been a bit frivolous in view of the hurry we were in.

But why were we hurrying?

CHAPTER 42

No Pursuit

We were all intent on the trip over the bridge and recovering the boards that we drove on. As soon as I was back in the wagon Virgil asked the question for both of us. "Are we in a hurry, Paw?"

Perhaps Mac did not realize his rush to take off was not usual. He looked quizzically down at his son. "Yes, I think it is best we be in a hurry, Virgil. I am not certain it is important, but to hurry seems right."

"Why,?" came the simple question.

"Well, the truth of the matter is there were Indians in the vicinity of the well. They did not know Joe and I were hidden there. We were fortunate that we had already bedded down for the night when they came to get their water. If we had been seen they may well have thought it was time for them to have some fresh meat.

"Remember how you kept a lookout for Indians when we found our Indian friend, Small Boy? Now we should keep a sharp lookout in the distance at some spot. Look carefully, then look away and count to five. Look back, find the spot, look at it carefully. Has it changed, or has the shadow near it changed? Maybe you could keep track of two spots for a while. If there are any Indians we might be better off to know about it and not be surprised."

"Why,?" came the direct question again.

"Indians think it is important to show no fear. I would rather have them think we are not afraid especially if they are wearing war paint. If we are not surprised by them it is easier to show no fear. What do you think you could do, Virgil, to make them think you are not afraid?"

The child was thoughtful. "Back home, Paw, you told me to remember to smile at strangers to make them feel friendly. I think I could do that. I could smile at the Indians, but I would not laugh at their war paint."

"That sounds good, Virgil. Now let's start looking for anything that changes or is different like a big extra lump on a bush."

To myself I thought it was all very well to be on the watch now but I wanted to find out what happened last night at the spring. How did Mac keep the Indians from knowing he was there? He says nothing now so Virgil won't be alarmed. But I am already alarmed and do hope I am able to turn on a smile at the proper time as Virgil said.

We all three quietly began the vigil for distant and near changes. It was entertaining after awhile, after I ceased to be afraid of what I might see. Virgil finally broke our silence with a little laugh as he said, "We are playing Hide-and-go-seek with the Indians only we don't know if they are hiding and they don't know we are seeking." Mac chuckled at his observations and it broke the tension of searching.

"Mac," I asked, "Tell us something about the Indians you saw last night."

"Not much to tell. The Lord surely was with me. I had gotten to the well before dark, fed and watered Joe and got him settled down behind some young saplings. I covered his tracks and mine before I crawled into the cave in the wall. You remember the caves there, don't you? Of course I did not start a fire. I was munching on my supper when I heard Indian voices, just a word or two. I even stopped chewing, I was so quiet. They were on foot, but I never knew how many were there. I heard only two voices and though their footsteps were light I thought there must have been about four people. They came for water and left soon after. Joe and I had a quiet night and were up this morning before first light. The waning moon gave just enough light to fill the water barrels but I could not see the visitors' footprints. I wanted to hurry back to your camp to make certain everything was all right here. And everything was all right except for one busted toe, eh, Virgil? How is it feeling now?"

Virgil wiggled his toe and said he thought it was getting better, then heaved a big sigh—big enough for me, too.

Mac had more time to ask about the toe. "Tell me, Virgil, how did it happen? You have been very careful all week."

"Yes," came the thoughtful reply. "Mama and I have been very careful. I wasn't even running but there were two of those thousand-legger varmints that were running and I couldn't hit them both. I tried to roll the rock I was holding so it would get one critter but the rock just landed on my toe instead. Both of the varmints got away. My toe sure did hurt but it didn't bleed very much."

"He was a very brave lad," I added. "Nary a tear."

"A fine boy," Mac added, patting his son's head.

CHAPTER 43

Arrival in Arizona Territory

September 29, 1865

A few days after we crossed the tree-lined Verde River Mac said we were getting close to our destination. It has been a long hot climb out of the valley. The higher we go the cooler the air has become and the nights are blessedly cool. Yesterday Mac said we'd reach our destination tomorrow, PROBABLY.

I think I sounded pleased at the prospect of ending our journey. But I am not at all certain I did for there was a great jumble of thoughts racing through my mind. First I thought, how can we suddenly end this way of life? We have been getting up every morning and scurrying off before dawn to be able to rest during the great heat of the day. We have led this nomadic life for so long that now I cannot believe I know how else to live.

Crowding in on these thoughts were those of propriety. What would it be like in the new town? Clean clothing had ceased to be a problem for me. How could I make a proper presentation of my family? I had for a long while looked like a gypsy who cared nothing for her appearance. I had given up being proud of my family's good grooming. As Keeper of the Flame I had stopped even thinking of my position of running a household properly.

Then I was shocked that all this veneer should come before the great relief of finally arriving alive at our destination. Thankfulness was the emotion that rose above these worries. Truly I was thankful to God that our health had held up. When I look back on how ignorant I was at the onset of our journey, of all the perils that befell us and the many more that we escaped, it was grateful, I was, that we were so near the end.

It must have been ten o'clock this morning when Virgil interrupted our thoughts with his expression of happiness. "My stomach has a happy squirming inside that we are really coming to the end of our trip to Arizona Territory."

"Yes," I agreed, "Your Papa is going to get a good rest at last."

We had crested a little hill when Virgil pointed ahead and asked, "What's that down there?"

Mac pulled on the oxen to stop then stroked his whiskers. "I do declare!" he exclaimed. "That has shore enough got to be our destination. You found it first, Virgil," and Mac slapped his old dusty hat on his knee in great glee.

I looked hard ahead and saw, finally, the pitiful little gathering of shelters below us. I didn't know whether to laugh or cry. "Oh," I managed to say, then pumped it up with a bit more enthusiasm, "Oh! It is a town. I see it through the trees." This was no time to cry. Plenty of time for that later on. "Oh there are trees, tall trees all about us!" I exclaimed with joy.

CHAPTER 44

The Wrestling Match

Mac drove us down the wide dusty road into town. I was mighty pleased I was wearing a sunbonnet to cover my browned face. Mac and Virgil were all agog to see what, where and who was about the town. They had no trouble finding out. Anyone who was inside a house or tent came out and all gawked as though they had never before seen a human being.

In front of a finished log building Mac pulled the oxen to a stop and alighted. Puffs of dust bloomed about his boots as he laid the lines over the hitching rail. Mac was greeted with smiles and handshakes by the men standing about. I did not hear what was said for my attention was drawn to the direction Virgil had gone and the conversation I heard at the rear of the wagon.

"Rassle down," was the first remark.

"No, you can't neither," came Virgil's loud, strong reply.

Then immediately came a few loud grunts and a jarring against a back wheel. I quietly left the seat and stepped through the wagon to look out back. There were two scuffling boys of about the same age rolling in the dust at the right wheel. At the left wheel stood a man dressed in work clothes with a grin on his face as big as a half moon. There came a voice from the dust at his feet. "Say uncle." "Uncle" was dutifully repeated. Two boys untangled their legs and stood up, wearing grins as big as the adults' standing over them.

"I see you met yore match, Willie," allowed the man. "Howdy do Ma'm," he then greeted me. "This here is my nephew, Will. He ain't rightly had nobody to do him any good in a rasslin' match for some time. He was about to get too big for his britches." Without expecting a reply from me he turned to the victor. "What be yore name, young man?"

Virgil wiped a dirty shirt sleeve across his smudged face without improving the situation and promptly answered, "Virgil McGinnis, sir." Then turning to me and smiling sweetly explained, "We's having a little fun, Mama."

"Ma'am," asked Will, lifting his well-freckled face to me, "May Virgil come see my yeller-legged, pink-spotted toad?"

The vanquished lad was all generosity. My thought was he can't likely get lost and these two will surely be just what each needs in the way of a friend.

"Yes, but mind you come the minute your Paw calls you, Virgil. Don't be gone far, Will."

I nodded to Will's uncle and stepped back into the wagon. I did not want to get into a conversation with a strange man. Well, I thought to myself, Virgil thinks this is a fine place to have landed. Now I wonder what Mac has found in the way of a place to live.

CHAPTER 45

Getting Settled in This House

I felt encouraged when Mac reported there was a dwelling available to us. I knew it would not be a mansion. I certainly did not expect one from the glimpse we had of the town as we drove down the main street. But this shelter tries my very soul. It has not been lived in since mid-summer. Not by human beings at least. Every other horrible creature known, with the exception of snakes, was here in abundance. Spiders, longlegs, scorpions, pack rats, mice, and thousand-leggers. Even the cunning chipmunks better stay out of my house. The day has been spent getting rid of the pests along with a fine layer of dirt and grit that had blown in. Now I find the critters are returning through the chinks in the logs!

The shelter is five logs high, with a double tent roof high enough for Mac to stand upright. I am grateful there is a canvas floor. Surely that is why the snakes had not slithered in. The 9-by-12-foot space inside is adequate for now. If only we can keep out the wild life until Mac builds a snug and tight-fitting cabin next spring.

Virgil is happy as a bumblebee and just as busy helping his Paw drive pegs in the wall to put up shelves. I am determined I will not weep over this excuse for a house for we are setting up housekeeping of a sort.

Last night we camped in our new half-log-cabin home. After our full day of cleaning it out we had time to unpack only part of the wagonload, and then cook meat and biscuits for supper. A kindly neighbor shared some venison steaks with us-—a purely thoughtful thing to do.

We were all tuckered out and slept well. When the coyotes howled in the night I awakened enough to know I was in a different place. Then a great peace flooded to my mind with the thought, "We are safe in town at last." That thought is surely the true sign of my acceptance.

My notion of this place being a big town with a store was a pure daydream, and I should have been more sensible. Perhaps I can even accommodate my mind to this being a dwelling we can accept and make into a home for a few months. Having a tent top gives a good light interior. I can easily see to thread a needle.

CHAPTER 46

Provisions

I had not thought to worry about provisions once we arrived here, since I expected this town to have merchants and stores. Now that we have awakened to real life, we need to make plans. Water is no longer a problem but nearly everything else is. Some thoughtful travelers brought seeds and grew gardens this past summer. Some things can be bought from them but not much considering their winter needs.

We have some flour, a bit of corn meal, very little bacon and some tea. Fresh meat is not too difficult to be had.

Already there is a plan. The miners have need of supplies that can be brought from California or closer. Mac will soon make a journey for them and bring us the provisions we need, and others need, as well. There will be another wagon and an Indian guide with him. I am thankful, but he will not be getting that rest I had spoken of.

Virgil is to remain here and be the-man-of-the-house, though his wish is to go with his Paw and help with the new span of mules Mac bought. Caring for our worn-out oxen is not to Virgil's liking.

In the meantime, school will be opening but not taught by a man, another disappointment. I must learn the two ladies' names. I heard tell one of them even has a small piano but that will not interest our lively boy.

Two weeks of Mac's absence will give me a bit of time to begin sewing the yard goods I bought in Santa Fe. My two men need shirts and I am not being too worldly to want another dress besides this old one. If I made a new bonnet it would not look too giddy if I trimmed it like a dress. I wonder if Mac would notice. If he does he will like it.

The weather has been the very best—a bit of breeze to keep the sun from being too hot and always cool at night. I am truly certain I will find more things to like about our town.

CHAPTER 47

Virgil's First Day at School

Last evening Virgil was surprised when I called him in early from his play. He knows better than to whine and beg so he asked me very respectfully if he might play until dark. I asked him if he had forgotten he was going to school tomorrow.

A strange look of first pain then pleasure crossed his face. "Oh, Maw, I guess I forgot for a bit. I have my new writing-figuring board Paw made for me and the charcoal holder, too."

"With all that fine equipment you surely can't go to school unless you are clean," I remarked.

"You mean I have to wash more than my face, hands and feet?" he questioned in surprise.

"Yes, and wash your hair first of all. The tub of water is already in the storage room. I laid out your night shirt there, too."

While he bathed I sat in the front doorway to finish hemming his new shirt I'd made, cut down from one of his Paw's.

Mac questioned, "Why such a big sigh?"

"Oh", I half laughed, not realizing I had revealed my inner thoughts. "I was thinking. Thinking that here we are—a wild town of mountain men and miners, California our nearest source of supply, but our children are not growing up ignorant and uncivilized. They are going to have an education and grow up refined men and women. You know the school is teaching music, too. Some of the men were against it but solid common sense won out.

"I think there are five, maybe seven, children on the roll. I presume all the boys will be barefoot since it is only early November. Later on Virgil can start wearing his new shoes you made for him. You are a good provider, Mac."

Mac rose and stretched. "I had better go see if Virgil is clean behind the ears."

Virgil's first day of school left my day strangely empty, a thing I had not excepted. But that is nothing. It is important, though, that we parents have provided a school for the children. The town is nearing two years old and our children need schooling. We want them to become refined ladies and gentlemen in spite of the mountain men, miners and gamblers that abound.

I was out in the dried bean patch when Virgil came home from school. He was climbing down from his bedroom loft when I entered the kitchen.

"Hello, Mama'" he greeted rather formally without his usual good cheer. "I knew you would want me to change to my play clothes. And I will wear them to school tomorrow, too, so I can play at recess."

"Well," I replied, "your play clothes are not very good looking clothes for school."

"They will do fine," said his father, entering at that moment.

There was a finality about Mac's comment so I changed the subject. "How was school today, Virgil?" My question caught him just before he left the house.

"Oh, I liked school, Mama. Mrs. Perkins has a real glass window in her kitchen just like Grandma's in Ohio. We all sat at the table and did our sums and our writing. Then we went out to play. Mrs. Perkins called that recess. That's when I decided I should have my play clothes on."

"Were all the boys wearing play clothes?"

"Yes," came the slow reply, "and they were playing "Crack the Whip" and I was on the end and I fell down. And and…"

I could tell the wistful voice was near to tears and more need not be said. "Well, I guess play clothes will be best. Better go get you shirt so I can wash it and have it ready for Sunday's wear."

Slowly Virgil returned, handed me the wadded up clothes as he looked up directly at my face and remarked, "I think they will need more than washing, Mama."

We heard Will calling to come play and Virgil hurried off.

Mac cleared his throat. I turned to him as I spread out the shredded garment. "Why, what…," Then I saw Mac could no longer suppress his laughter, and he began the explanation of the torn shirt.

"I had driven the team up to the school just at closing time. Virgil's shirt looked dirty as he came out the schoolhouse door but it looked worse in short order. A bigger boy spun Virgil around and ripped his shirt down the back, then said something. Virgil waited not an instant but piled into that boy's belly with both fists."

"Why!" I exclaimed horrified, but Mac continued.

"It didn't last long. Just long enough for Virgil to trip up the boy, sit on his neck and yell, 'Say Uncle.' It was all over in a jiffy, even before the younguns had a chance to call out, 'Fight, fight!'

"Virgil hadn't noticed my team standing there. I drove onto Gurley and came up even with the school younguns and offered a ride to anyone. Virgil hopped up beside me, greeted me cheerfully, and said, 'Thanks for the figurin' board, Paw. That boy over there said he was gonna take it away from me but I said he wasn't.'

"So, Virgil had a pretty fair day, his first day in school. Next time it may be different." Mac rubbed his whiskers and grinned as he reflected on the possibilities.

My thoughts of refined ladies and gentlemen were left to the future.

CHAPTER 48

Molly's Silent Conversation With Mac

(A private Journal Entry)

Is there news of the wagon train? Has no messenger come from St. Louis? You say I'll know of their arrival soon enough when a column of dust signals their position. Yes, the choking dust, I remember it well as we journeyed westward. We sometimes had pleasant days. They followed the storms, storms intent on blowing us, rolling us like tumbleweeds that suddenly washed in thundering roar down a once dry arroyo. We did sidestep that flood and then the mud that gripped the wagon wheels to the axles. How often did we lighten our load before the straining oxen could inch us forward? Men shouting their orders in blasphemous bellows, the cracking of whips, the groaning at the pry-poles, all increased the effort that freed us. Could I endure the journey again? Which is the greater agony, returning to civilization or the life of fear and privation in our new home on Granite Creek?

You're announcing three more for supper? Yes, I suppose there's stew enough in the pot. They've returned from the Walker party? Gone from the camp for more than three weeks? You call them shinn-warmers. That's easy enough. I say they know their own hearts, I give them that. You say they think it takes courage to live in the wilderness. No, just indifference. Indifference to everything but the search for gold. Yes, they came for adventure and gold-seeking, too. But they did not come for the killings. They left the hopeless havoc in the East, the war-torn, heart-battered families, farmlands in need of care, lying fallow. Their leaving was a kind of crying out for peace, a deep desire for sensible living, not furniture used as firewood. They knew the agony of brother fighting brother and turned from it with revulsion. With personal sacrifice and self-reliance they turned from comfortable scenes of childhood, the security of a business well started, grieving families, war's horror. They came for adventure? Well, perhaps, but not the repeated agony of more deaths, not this senseless strife with the Indians.

Yes, you say, the Indians should not kill, then they would not be threatened, that they are the ones guilty of torturing. But whose homeland is being disrupted, the very food for their families chased away or slaughtered with fine disregard? Have we taken any care that the Indian children have not suffered? None that I have heard of. It's still bullets, dying and grieving. I heard you. It's our lives balanced against the naked savages. But they have homes and families to protect, don't forget. That is what these young Confederates are remembering, too. This is the anguish they came to forget.

I need your permission to leave here? This is true, but I need the courage to leave, too. How can I stay here in any case? You do not know the revulsion within me. I fear the Indian raids at any untoward sound. Who can have a night of peace? I welcome dawn's slant of light. The morning sun from blazing blue thaws my frozen sleep. But do I dare venture from my flapping tent? Will it be an arrow whizzing at my head, or a fat, loathsome rattler at my heels?

President Lincoln declared us Arizona Territory. Has that improved this life since nearly a year ago? We still have no certain food supply, but a certainty there will be hunger. Soldiers are at hand, and so is Indian trouble. Treaties are beginning again, you say. Will they outlast a drunken prospector's anger? Of course the Indians have Firewater, and who but a greedy merchant sells it to them?

Truly I see little hope in this development here, and my wish is to be far from it. I long for us to be gone, yet you expound the growing plans for this pitiful group of tents. This town's growth is beginning, you say, as Territorial Capital it will go forward. This group of flapping tents remain the capital? Do you think the miners will stop seeking gold and build wooden structures? You believe our neatly surveyed square will be surrounded by business buildings? I can believe Governor Goodwin will succeed in calling a legislature together, I can believe his flapping tent, held down by his iron safe, will be replaced by a sturdy wooden structure, and one for Judge Allyn, too, but a row of business houses I cannot believe. If it is to be a town we do need them but the miners, will they exchange pickaxes and shovels for hammer and nails even if the saw-mill is a reality? I doubt that. Look, the free-flowing saloon is but a well-trod-den space under the Juniper tree. Truly I see no future here. I beg of you, let us leave. I hear your reply, "A place of the future must have a place of its beginning. We will remain here."

I have just read my last entry and am ashamed of such poor spirits. Father warned me there would be such times. I have never told him of the other trials that dogged our path last summer as we struggled on our westward journey nor shall I mention this one nor the ones I am convinced will follow. I must remember all we have to be thankful for.

We have now had a good soaking rain for two days. Besides cooling things off I have some hopes for the garden.

Mac is planning to build up a hauling service from California to the miners hereabouts and any others of this area who need such a service. He is certain that it will be useful and necessary. He is certain it will bring him more income than being a blacksmith. That may be, but I know he will be in greater danger out on the trail than in the blacksmith shop. His mind is made up.

CHAPTER 49

November Weather

November is here. Evenings have grown cooler and the sun slides earlier each day behind the western hills. The days have remained warm with little breeze. Yellow leaves sway gently scattering their soft gold onto the ground. This brilliant blue sky is the same that covered us as we traveled this past summer. The sun is bright but the searing heat is gone.

These days are complete enchantment. At times I cannot regret coming to Prescott. Mac warns me this weather will not last through the winter months. Not in Prescott, only farther south in Yuma. It would be strange to have no seasonal change. Mac experienced such during the Civil War and says he likes winter months and snow. Of course Virgil does too. Already he's asking for a sled at Christmas.

CHAPTER 50

The Red Yarn from Thanksgiving

There's the pumpkin and venison given by the Indian.
Strange, that Indian,
And red yarn in his braids.
Virgil said 'twas from his little red wagon
that Paw made.
Virgil gave the yarn to the Indian
the same day I fetched Virgil from the creek.
Quiet as a bird's wing that Indian appeared.
Though startled, Virgil smiled as told to do. Would
the Indian take him away? No, he reached only for the
yarn and felt it.
The child, so trusting and understanding,
To the Indian he handed the yarn.
A smile was returned,
The stoic Indian smiling at a little child.
Truly a lesson. "A little child shall lead them."
We have more than a pumpkin and venison
To give thanks for.
On Mac's return his pride in Virgil
Will shine like the morning sun.

Cold Tent Weather

Winter temperatures have come as Mac said they would. Living in a barracks tent is all right when the weather is favorable, but it is favorable no longer. The low log walls and double canvas top are poor protection in this severe cold and vicious wind.

The little stove gives off enough heat to make soup or heat water but is not sufficient for comfortable living.

Mac is away on a miners' supply trip in California. He surely would not have ventured out had he known this kind of weather was on the way. Of course he may not have the same fierce winds assailing him on his journey. He says California is milder than this place. Here the frozen trees creak and crack and limbs are falling. No tall trees are near our tent so we are not in danger that way. Pray God no trees fall or limbs strike Mac or his outfit. What a calamity that would be.

I am ashamed that I cried a bit yesterday. Today there shall be nary a trace. My, my! A grown woman feeling sorry for herself. My mother would be surprised at me. Never would I allow Virgil to see such a thing.

Mac has left us a goodly supply of wood and Virgil is my man-of-the-house and keeps the woodbox filled. Truly I just never thought we would have to bear up under such weather. In all last summer's miserable heat I never once thought there could come an equally killing cold. I had always thought there was no such weather in the south. Well, I have learned we are not really very far south.

Bless Governor Goodwin! We have just now had a messenger from him. He has brought us word that we are to sleep in the Governor's Mansion during this severe weather. I thanked the officer kindly and replied we would try one more night in the tent. How very kind! That was when I cried a wee tear. Someone did care and was mindful of our comfort.

At the close of school, when Virgil was home, the messenger returned with team and wagon and insisted we bring our bedding and come now. It was to be another very cold night and he could not take no for an answer. Then I realized we should accept the kindly offer. I took some of our wilted potatoes, and cold cornbread. They will help out. We took the feather tick and two heavy quilts, too.

The Governor's Mansion, as we named it, is a large four-room, spacious log building with two large fireplaces. At least twenty-five people were brought in out of the storm. There was room, as well as food, for all.

Mrs. Goodwin has returned to the East because of poor health. I think she overworked in the hot summer while setting out her beautiful yellow rose garden. She had brought the roses all this long journey and was not intending anything disastrous should happen to them. She surely worked too hard.

The good governor was most gracious and thoughtful of us all. After supper was cleared away by the help, we had a jolly time singing, telling tales of our traveling adventures and generally becoming acquainted.

Governor Goodwin's secretary, Mr. Richard McCormick, brought a book from his library. The author was the well-known historian, William Hickling Prescott. Mr. McCormick asked if we would enjoy hearing about the ancient Indian culture farther south.

We were soon entranced with tales of the famous Aztec chieftain, Montezuma. He was a warrior, lawgiver, as well as designer and director of temple buildings and pyramids in Mexico City. He directed the building of roads and highways to connect his people that they might exchange produce and goods. Some Aztec roads are in use today though they were built before the time of Columbus.

Soon members of our small gathering were asking Mr. McCormick questions showing much interest in the ancient neighbors to the south, but our children were falling asleep in our laps. We needed to tend to them and lay out our beds over the bearskin rugs that covered the mansion's floor.

We thanked Mr. McCormick and let him know we would like to hear more another time. It was the beginning of the decision to give the name Prescott to our little growing town, the capital of Arizona Territory.

The name decided on, I might add, was far superior to the one being bandied about. Because of numerous donkeys having been turned loose by departing miners the remaining miners preferred the uncouth name of Jack Ass Flats. Not at all amusing.

CHAPTER 52

Food Exchange with the Indian

The wind blew in a beautiful little snowstorm while Virgil and I and the other guests slept comfortably on our feather ticks laid over bear skin rugs on the floor of the governor's cozy home.

The smell of coffee and bacon aroused us to the new day. Good host that he was, Governor Goodwin insisted we roll our bedding against the wall for another night's stay out of the cold. We gladly accepted the invitation and the hearty breakfast as well.

Virgil was ready to go home at once, but only because he could not wait to get out in the snow. He was anxious to try the new boots Mac had made for him. He can't wait to tell his Paw how wonderful they are. The other children had already gone with their parents.

I needed to go back to our tent to make certain we were not raided in the night. By the time we were on our way home the sun had come out warmly. The snow was not melting but the cold wind blew it about leaving a few bare spots. The few inches of snow did not greatly inconvenience us. Virgil had great fun making snowballs for all the targets about him.

We found the tent in good order with nothing amiss. I do have a divided feeling about the Indians near us. We know some of them and feel they can be trusted and we can depend on them. Others come in who have no feelings of friendship. We remain friendly and are grateful that there are Indians who are watchful for our safety. The soldiers at Fort Whipple are a source of comfort but they cannot be at our side constantly.

❈   ❈   ❈

We have slept at the mansion for three nights now. Last night was not quite so cold. If it warms up to 20 degrees we will begin staying at home. This morning when we arrived at the tent I thought there were fresh footprints outside the door. I directed Virgil to bring in a few sticks of wood for a fire. I did not want him to enter the tent before I did. I was carrying two empty baskets and slung them into the tent ahead of me on either side of the doorway. They seemed not to meet with any obstacle so I bravely entered and found all was well. I thanked the dear Lord no one was inside.

In the little stove we found a few glowing coals among yesterday's ashes. Soon smoke was flowing up the chimney and the teakettle was warming. In a while an Indian came by asking for bread. He is one we know and I gladly gave him part of a loaf. He brought us a skinned rabbit. Certainly a fair exchange. Today I will bake bread and we'll have rabbit stew to take to the supper at the Mansion.

It is too difficult to ask questions of the Indian so I did not inquire if he had been to the door earlier. The Indians we know are so like little children who have no training, yet they show gentle kindness and a quickness in learning.

CHAPTER 53

Molly's Family

Smoke is rising on the still air.
Cookfires are rekindled, breakfast prepared.
The tent city is well astir.
Sun has rounded its turn at the horizon.
Virgil is warming his feet at the potbellied stove,
Too warm yet to wear shoes,
Too cold for comfort,
He stands close for scant warmth.
The waning fire has cooked cornpone,
Warmed the venison,
And heated Monday's wash water.
On the wooden scrub board
I rub the clothes in steady rhythm.

Virgil munches a piece of corn pone.
A request to play at the creek
Is answered by a glance at the empty water bucket
Needing to be filled first.
Boy with bucket bounces merrily off.

Straightening to rest a bit.
My thoughts idle my hands

and the past presents its mental pageant,
Envelops my world
Where I had walked in years past.
"Desert Arizona?" Mother had repeated, bewildered.
"Arizona's a desert," Father warned.
"Virgil is so young to leave us," pleaded Granny.
"Arizona is not all desert
and Virgil is a big boy,"
pronounced Grandpa, the scholar.
He stood steadfast as always
Like a great spreading oak
Giving me shelter when I was uncertain, when I
Chose not to be swayed by stronger opinions,
When family inclined me to go their way.
I married Mac and would gladly follow him.
Arizona was a long way and desert there was
But I craved some kind of freedom at last.

Smiling wryly, I return to scrubbing, remembering
how the family had towered over me. Father, from his
pulpit, a great unbending spruce,
raising his arms wide, encouraging,
yes, demanding, all come with him,
his direction, his decision,
his interpretation was right.
Even dancing,
there was nothing wrong with dancing,
joyful dancing in the bible was not wrong.
Mother at the piano waited patiently
for Father's direction to play.
Her fingers swayed delicately above the keys.
Her gentle movements like willow
that gives little shelter
but a lovely sight to see.
Dear Mother, so beautiful, dutiful to Father,
A quiet lady of culture.
Granny, sweet Granny, chair bound now, propped
with pillows like fruit-tree limbs needing help,

having born more than their share
of what life had to offer.
And I? I have rolled away from it all,
a tumbleweed in the wind.
But the trees are here, too,
Great Ponderosa trees, with the strength of Mac,
the wind singing through their high tops.
A good life will be made here.
A panting boy set a splashing bucket of water
at my feet.
Grinning, he waits for me to see the green frog
In the bottom of the bucket.

CHAPTER 54

Virgil's Dream

Though I had been listening I did not hear Virgil's feet above, padding across his loft floor. Paw is away so Virgil will not hear the familiar, "Let's hear those feet talk to the floor." I made aplenty of stove-lid and pot-clatter noises to rouse him out, but only silence from above.

Finally, a muffled sound. He must have had his head under the cover. Then a few oh's and at last a wail, "Oh Grandma." He was dreaming. Soon I heard snuffles, knew he was awake and crying over something from his dream.

I called out cheerily, "Good morning Virgil. Is there a sun shining up there?"

"No," came a grumpy reply.

"Peek through a crack. You will be sure to find at least one sun shining." His father insists I humor Virgil too much, but I really don't.

"Mama," came a petulant whimper, "I was having a nice dream and it ended before I was ready. It wasn't finished, and it ended," he wailed. "I wanted some more of that dream."

"Come on down and tell me about it," I invited. "Don't forget to spread up your bed."

There were movements above and the harsh rustling of the corn husk mattress, then two barefeet on the ladder.

"Good morning," I greeted. "The cornmeal mush is just ready to boil. You'll have time to wash and tell me about the dream before you forget it." I passed him the comb for his tousled hair. He took it and a dipper of water outside to the washbench. Inside again he declared, "Mama, I am not never going to forget that dream. It was about Grandma."

I did not correct him, he was so in earnest. "Mama, it was the nicest dream. She was wearing her pretty blue dress that she wears when she is doing the wash."

That memory came close to my heart, too. I smiled, patted his head as he continued. "Even if she did have her wash dress on we were going to church. Grandma asked me to come up in the attic with her to help find something in the big trunk. You remember Grandma has stairs to her attic, don't you?" How could I forget! "Oh Mama, it was such a good dream. I could see Grandma's fat fingers like little pillows and her pretty gold ring, too. She already had her hat on so I could not see her white hair except around the edges. It looked so pretty where it touched her cheeks. I wish Grandma was still alive."

It seemed like a good time for me to stir the mush. This dream was real for me, too. "Go on," I encouraged.

"Well, there were a lot of things in the attic that I don't think are really there. One long box was about four foot long." "Feet," I corrected.

"Feet," he agreed, "and it had a peeked-roof lid on it. She closed it without even looking in the box." Her wedding dress and gloves I thought, and brushed away a tear.

"I could see the big trunk where we were going to get something to take to church so the pew would not be so hard. I think Grandma said it was a velvet cloak. I had never seen that before. We were almost over to the trunk. I could see the brass nail heads on the bands that ran over the big humped back of the trunk. I could hardly wait for us to open the lid. And, Mama, that's when I wakened…before the dream was finished! Why do dreams do that?"

"There was the pleasure of the beginning," I smiled sympathetically. "Who knows why they end abruptly?" I shook my head, still caught up in the dear memories of the trunk and the attic, so far away and long ago.

CHAPTER 55

The Dust Rag

Life in Prescott has improved since our arrival here a year ago in 1865. My great anticipation and joy is our snug log cabin which Mac is building. It is Mac's greatest pleasure and pride. Hard work and privations have been ours a plenty but daily life has become less worrisome. Ft. Whipple has re-established itself 25 miles nearer by for greater protection from the Indians. The Army had mistaken another landmark that resembles Thumb Butte, so they originally made camp where the soldiers were not useful to the miners and settlers of Prescott. Miners' protection comes first, of course.

The morning sun in the bright blue sky discourages frowns and complaints. This day, however, I was aggravated at the outset, but it all ended in a laugh. I could not find my dust rag anywhere. I hang it on a peg with the dustpan Mac whittled for me. I finally quit wasting my time searching, found another rag that would do as well and got to work. But that favorite cloth did not entirely leave my mind.

With the housework done I took some potatoes out to peel while I sat on the stoop. I intended cooling off before starting the supper. Virgil was out playing near the stone fence. He still had the little fire shovel he had asked to use. I called to him and he came running to sit and visit with me. I was pleased that he had remembered to bring the tool with him.

"Did you know your paw made that shovel when he first learned to forge metal? He was about your age, maybe three years older. He was ten. Boys had to work much harder in those days. Were you digging up a place to plant something?" I asked.

Virgil's head turned quickly toward me and searched my face. "No, I wasn't exactly planting." His chin dropped and he looked toward the end of the steps.

I looked in the same direction. "What did you dig for at the steps?"

Virgil stood, not answering my question, and remarked, "I'll go put the shovel away."

"What did you find when you dug here?" I persisted.

"Nothing," he mumbled. "I wasn't looking for nothing."

"Anything," I corrected. "It's hard work to dig under the steps. Why did you decide to dig there?"

"I thought I had to," he mumbled and moved a bit farther away.

Now I began to get curious. "Did you think I wanted you to dig under the steps?" I asked softly. Glancing toward him I saw a tear roll down his cheek. I reached my hand out to him and suggested, "Tell me all about it."

He took a step toward me, laid his head on my shoulder and burst into tears. "Mama, I'm sorry. I took your cleaning rag. I wanted it to make my warts go away. I didn't think you would care about that old rag. I wasn't stealing it but I'm not supposed to ask for it. I was to take it, rub my warts with it then go bury it under the steps. They haven't gone away yet."

He sobbed so hard I could scarcely understand his tale, but knew it by heart myself. "There, there," I comforted him. "We'll just see if they go away." I thought to myself it would be interesting to see if the charm worked with a dust rag as well as a dishrag. Then I told Virgil the story of my own wart that had gone away when I rubbed it with a grain of corn and dropped the corn into the well as my Paw had whispered for me to do.

Virgil wiped his face on his shirtsleeve, grinned faintly as he stood to put away the treasured shovel. "They'll go away," he said. "The dust rag will do it, too. Your Paw just tells you and it works."

CHAPTER 56

The Tribes

Virgil had been sitting on the door step in a pensive mood ever since we returned home from church services. Finally I inquired what was on his mind.

"Mama, do you remember Little Cloud? Could Little Cloud read?"

Virgil is ten years old now. It is four years since we said good-bye to our good Indian friend. Of course I remember him well. We never have heard news of him since we crossed the Mississippi River at Keokuk, Iowa and he returned to his family in Ohio. I wondered what was on Virgil's mind.

"Well, I am not really certain Virgil. I had no occasion to see or hear him read. I know he had a copy of the Holy Bible so perhaps he could read. Why do you ask?"

"I was just wondering if Indians learn to read like we do, in books, besides the Bible?"

"Do you mean are Indians able to learn to read?"

"Yes, and do they have books in their language?"

"Before the Spanish priests came to this part of the world the Indians did not have books because they did not have a language that was written down. So of course they did not read. They had special men who were the story tellers of their clan whose job it was to remember everything and teach the children what they had to know. There were a great many things to learn. The stories were told over many times and so the children learned them. I suppose they teach their children the same way now.

Today Little Cloud may read to his children but he probably could not read more than the Bible. There are no books for all the things his children must learn in their Indian life. The Indians who live near us do not have books for the same reason. What do you think about it?"

"Well, I guess Indians do not read if they don't have books and I think they may not have much use for books. But, Mama, they do know lots of things, Indians do. I wish I could make arrow heads."

CHAPTER 57

The Log Cabin

I went with Mac yesterday to the cabin site. I sat in the shade knitting while the men were laying the sills on the foundation walls, notching the sleepers and the logs for our new cabin. Notching and pegging require exact work if the floors are to be level and the walls are not to lean. A few auger holes will be necessary and I was surprised to learn that square pegs make a tighter fit in the round holes.

Mac cannot do the work alone. He is most grateful to Jim Lamb for the main planning of the work. In Ohio Mac never was so engaged. His blacksmith shop kept him occupied from dawn to dark. Right now this cabin-building is his whole life and he is learning so many new things. Though tired at night he has been dressing the shingles he split out last fall. It makes lovely shavings for the woodbin and keeps Virgil busy with picking up. He prefers the easier job of picking up the auger curls. Either way, it is easier than having to split the kindling for the fire.

The work on the cabin has improved Virgil's numbering and ciphering. He has been keen to watch the measurement centers of the sleepers and reports these quite accurately to me. He is quick to learn and eager to be with the men. He is yet too young to use the ax in accurate work but he whittles away at the high spots in the log notches. The dovetail notching that really holds the logs firmly takes more careful work than even Mac can do. Here Mr. Lamb's expert ax work is needed. Virgil is allowed to drive the pegs into the auger holes a little way but cannot complete the job. Two or three strokes are all he is allowed for the peg must go in straight. He at least has a knowing of his worth.

I heard Mr. Lamb tell Mac that he was wise to have floor boards of 6-inch depth for extra winter warmth. Prescott winters are not always as warm as last winter. My thought was that if they were to be any colder perhaps we should double the floor's depth. Of course I jest. The winter was not truly too severe. I think not having expected to live during the winter in a tent with half-wooden walls was part of the discomfort. I look forward with joy to spend this coming winter in a cabin with a wooden floor, not a canvas one with fur throw rugs. Mother and Father need not be distressed thinking we live poorly in a tent. I think of the cabin as quite grand. True comfort is living in a solid shelter for the winter. It is sized just right for us, 16'-by-24'. Nothing like the Governor's Mansion, of course. Mac even plans to bring us a glass window from California on his next supply trip for the miners.

First things must come first and getting the cabin up is certainly first. But such a clutter of limbs we have about us yet. Some of the limbs must be burned to get them out of the way but many can be cut by Virgil for winter firewood and the twigs for early fire of a morning. Many limbs will be just right when sawed to fireplace length. What a wealth of supply we will have.

Virgil pretends he is wrangling horses when he tugs at the limbs he is able to move. In his letter to his grandparents he carefully wrote out the words, "I can work." I told them of his many chores. He has gathered a great pile of pine cones that will be handy for starting up the morning fire in winter. Pine needles, too, he has piled with a brush broom.

I never think of pine needles as part of the clutter. They have so pleasant a scent as they are walked on. Just be careful on a hill for they are slippery, too. Virgil thinks sliding on the needles is as much fun as sledding in the snow.

I find I am developing more kindly feelings for Prescott when treading on these scented, soft needles. I am casting off my longings for home. No, I must not say "home" when I think of Ohio. I shall think "back there" or "in the East." This is home now, Prescott. This is where we live. I find I think less and less of ever returning. We are established here. Mac is particularly satisfied in his service of providing supplies for the miners.

Recently Mac explained to me how he plans to later build an addition onto the cabin for storing miners' supplies. It will someday be an entrance for a true extension of the cabin.

I cannot think that far ahead. A loft room for Virgil with a true stairs going up and a wooden floor are all the dreams I have. I can scarcely wait to have the floor thickly covered with pine needles and neatly covered over with the new rag carpets I've been weaving. That will be grand, indeed. Mac says he will not forget about a true glass window the next time he travels to California. I will be patient with oiled paper in the meantime.

Our cabin is situated on a little knoll for good drainage. It is a lesson we learned last fall when the rain came down so hard it made a river flowing under and around us. What a problem we had to keep the mud from underfoot. I want none of that in this cabin.

Such a muddy condition there is on Gurley Street, Cortez, and Montezuma. Last week Virgil and I rode in the wagon with Mac when he went to town. It was a treat to get out for a bit, but Mac would not drive the team onto Gurley Street beyond Marina. I didn't get to see the stores but waited in the wagon until my two men returned from buying. It would have been no pleasure to be out in that mess. The mud was almost up to the wagon axles. While waiting I saw a puppy that wanted to cross the road. At the edge of the board walk he stopped, lifted a paw, almost put it down in the mire, then turned and trotted off. It was too much for even a dog.

When Prescott mud dries onto boots, or any surface, it dries hard as a rock. Plainly it is why the Indian women are successful in making bowls using this clay. There is some good in everything. I wonder if I could make clay pots and bowls.

That is not what Virgil wonders. He wonders if he could have a dog. Perhaps later. We are busy enough growing and preparing food and putting some by for the winter for us three. I doubt there would be enough scraps to feed a hungry dog. Later on we can manage it. At present there are plenty of dogs about to give warning or protection.

CHAPTER 58

Lament in the Potato Patch

Today I labored mightily. Mac is away on a supply trip in California. Cold weather has set in, and since he has gone, of course I must harvest the potatoes before the ground freezes. What a miserable job it is. If I wait for rain to soften the ground, the clay sticks to my hoe until I scarce can lift it. If the ground is dry it is so hard I am likely to break the hoe's blade. Truly, a pick like the miners use would be the best tool for the job.

As I worked away at my back-breaking task I was thinking of that dear soul we met on the prairie last summer. Alice was her name. She had a far more difficult garden problem. It is possible for me to dig down into this baked and rocky soil to plant, weed or harvest, even if I need a pick instead of a hoe.

Out on the prairie she had to dig through a tough matt of grass roots to plant or weed. When harvest time came it was a rock-hard mass to cut through again. But she did say the soil was rich and produced a heavy crop providing there was enough rain.

I wonder sometimes how the good Lord expects us to provide for ourselves. I do not mean to blaspheme for I would be struck down. But we struggle so hard, then the grasshoppers come and eat everything in sight. Or chinch bugs ruin the hay. Or a late frost kills the new plant growth and it is too late to plant again and bring the crop to maturity. We till in the rocks, the clay, the matted roots and then no rain falls. So much of our work is futile.

The Indians have a fine system of irrigating since there is bound to be a lack of summer rain. We seem to insist on planting where we cannot irrigate. Or planting things that will not grow here. Perhaps we should live as simply as the

Indians do. But I should not like to live on only squash, cornmeal and beans and have no potatoes through the winter. So we wail about our problems.

These are a miserable size of potato. Father would say they are not worth picking up. Perhaps he is right but it is the food we will have for the winter. I am thankful we have it though I wonder, is it worth this aching back of mine.

Later in the Day

I am trembling so violently I scarce can hold the pen to write. I am ashamed to be so upset, but a snake has that effect on me every time.

Little good it did me to have the hoe in my hand; I flung it away in a wide arc. Never could I have made use of it way over where it landed. The dish of ready-sprouted beans, which I was carrying, I had sense enough to hold onto. At least I did not scream; I can be proud of that.

That I nearly stepped on the creature is the thing that frightened me most. Usually they slither off and you see them at a safe distance. But this little thing, and it was only about ten inches long, was coiled into a tight knot and my foot nearly landed on top of him.

As I flung the hoe away from me, my feet, all on their own, did a quick, little two-step dance in place. The fact that I did not advance kept the snake from being trampled. Had I stepped on that squirming mass I am certain my scream could have been heard in Ohio.

I have settled myself a bit and can think back to the scene now. I realize the snake was neatly banded with black and brilliant orange, ending with an orange nose. A thing of beauty if they were not such creepy creatures. But beautiful or not, the beans can be planted tomorrow.

Since Mac is away he will not hear my new wail, and I am determined I will not cry, neither now nor when he returns. He is inclined to think I complain a bit too much. The Indians are his great problem as he journeys to California for his orders of goods. He has had but little trouble for he uses the "magic signs and words" that Little Cloud taught him long ago.

Should Mac have the trials and tribulations that are mine I know he would say they are naught. Naught they may be but when a two-inch bug, with feelers two inches longer on each side of its head, lands right on the bean I am ready to pick it is certainly something to be reckoned with. It looked like a long-horned steer with wings.

I called, really I yelled in a most unladylike way, and Virgil came running. To him it was a treasure and a delight that he can show to his friends. To me it is just another varmint that will be the finish of the few vegetables that have managed to escape the grey beetles, the black bugs, the sucking aphids, and the rabbits. My wailing problems, Mac calls them. It is truly serious to me for I must have the food to can and put by for winter.

CHAPTER 59

Dinner for One

I did the unthinkable today. I went back to sleep and slept until sunup. Since Mac is away I will be the only one who suffers. I will have to do the garden work in the hot sun, something that never bothers Virgil.

The two of us were out before the dew dried, hauling our garden water from the creek. Virgil thinks it is a day lost if he doesn't get to walk barefoot in the dewy grass. There is precious little grass in this hot dry spell. Even the weeds are giving us less trouble.

We had poured the water carefully in our irrigation ditches and had just begun the weeding when the birds began a dreadful squawking, at least the jays did. I paid them little heed but Virgil, ever curious, watched their antics.

Finally he said with certainty, "There's something in the little oak tree that they are upset about and I can see one little bird fanning its wings and not going anywhere. I'm going over to have a look, Mama."

Virgil approached the scene of his curiosity carefully but the jays flew away and squawked at a distance. Finally I was inquisitive enough that I called over to ask what he found. I wanted Virgil to come on back to work.

"Mama, I want to watch awhile," he called, his voice showing keen interest.

I walked over to see what could be so important and Virgil warned me, "Mama, you may not want to see this. It's a snake in the tree."

When I questioned if it was safe and I'd not be bitten he assured me it was perfectly safe and then added, "The snake has his mouth full and he can't bite anything more. Besides, he's just a little racer snake and couldn't hurt you anyway."

About that I was not certain but went over to see what was so fascinating. At first I was frightened and revolted, too. Then I came to see it was one of God's creatures eating, as it was supposed to do.

Virgil told me later that he was very proud of me for not making a fuss over the snake eating the bird.

"When that snake stretched his mouth and then stretched it some more until he could swallow the first bite I thought sure you would take the bird away from him. And Mama I thought the snake would never be able to stretch over the birds wings even if it was just a little sparrow. But God gave the snake permission to eat a bird if he could catch it. So the snake knew he could do it."

"Did you notice the other little birds come?" I asked.

"They were getting their lesson on what to be careful about as they landed in the trees. All twigs are not alike. We all have our lessons to learn."

CHAPTER 60

Punishment

Virgil stuck his head in at the door and called, "We're going to water the garden."

That was all and the door closed. Knowing he was not wearing his good shoes I had no complaints. However, it was a hearty choice of fun for him and his friend, Kenny, who had come to play.

Kenny's sister, Genevee, came in soon after. She was brushing at her skirt and snuffing from a slight crying spell. I didn't say anything for I thought if she had fallen she was big enough to take a tumble without too much fuss made over it. She hung her coat and cap on the peg near the door.

As she passed me I asked, "Did all the dust come off?"

"Yes, Ma'am, thank you," and she nodded her pretty red-golden curls as she picked up some quilt pieces I was working with.

She chose a needle and was soon occupied. We made small conversation about her being a big girl in first grade. She liked going to school. She and Kenny walk to school in town from Miller Valley. She didn't like missing when it rained or snowed hard. Sometimes they caught a ride to town in a horse-drawn wagon; an oxen team was too slow. But usually the road was so rough they walked rather than be bumped about in the empty wagon. If it was loaded with bags of feed it wasn't so bad. A load of lumber did not make for much comfort either. "And," she added, "I'm always afraid I'll fall off the high pile of lumber and spill my dinner bucket."

Outside we heard a great stomping of feet accompanied by hilarious laughter. The two boys came in with rather composed faces that broke into broad grins as they glanced at each other. Virgil stepped over to the water bucket to take a gulp from the dipper. On the second gulp he dropped the dipper and dashed for the door. Cheeks puffed out, he was convulsed with laughter and barely made it to the steps before he spouted water before him. Kenny was close behind him and both of them were doubled over with merriment.

I smiled at Genevee and asked what could be the cause for such a circus.

"Well, I don't know," was her prim reply. "It wasn't very funny while I was out there."

Wondering what deviltry those two had been up to I asked what had happened.

"Oh, the boys climbed over the fence into the goat's yard. I went over the stile. As I turned to watch the boys the billy goat ran at me from behind and butted me down. The boys had a big laugh over that, but they did drive off Billy and helped brush me off and said they were very sorry. Didn't make me feel much better though."

I expressed my shock and sympathy and inquired if she was feeling all right. She assured me she was and went with me to the door to see what the boys were doing.

Right away I saw the rain barrel on its side, against the shed, at the bottom of the hill. Virgil was not in sight but I called to him to get the barrel back up under the downspout or his Paw would be upset.

Around the corner the two of them came, still doubled up with laughter.

"Virgil," I said perplexed, "What is so funny?"

"Oh, Mama," he tried to speak and doubled over again while I waited patiently.

"Well,the goat," began Kenny, and he doubled over in spasms.

"Now, boys, that goat butting Genevee down was not that funny. Straighten up."

"Yes, Mama," began Virgil seriously. "It was not one bit funny. We felt bad that poor Genevee was hurt. When she started to the house Kenny and I decided to punish the goat. So we watered the garden to empty the water out of the rain barrel. We put some turnips in the barrel. When the goat put his head in to eat we shoved him all the way into the barrel and rolled it down the hill."

Again the boys doubled up in laughter. What was so funny?

"Oh, Mama! When the goat finally scrambled all the way out of the barrel he was so dizzy. Oh it was so funny, Mama. He floundered and staggered and fell over sideways when he tried to walk." Virgil gave a dizzy, staggering dance to imitate the goat. "When he tried to stand he'd shake his head and fall down again. He fell down all the time, Mama. Finally he sat there just like a dog, only swaying back and forth ready to fall over again. I wish you could have seen him."

While the boys enjoyed their joke Genevee and I looked at each other and we laughed too, both at the laughing boys and the thought of the dizzy goat, who got his punishment.

CHAPTER 61

Christmas Thoughts

Virgil has been in a pensive state the last day or so. Finally I asked him what was on his mind.

"Well, Mama, I was thinking about the Christmas story. About the Baby Jesus and his Mother Mary and about the Baby Jesus being born in a manger. I know you told me things were different now than in Jesus' day, but I've been wondering about it."

"Yes," I encouraged him and wondered what was coming next.

"Well, when Mrs. Santigo had her baby you had me pump buckets and buckets of water for her. Did Joseph pump water for Mary?"

I must admit that was something I had never thought of in all my life but it was something I could answer.

"Yes, Virgil, you were a big help. You pumped three buckets of water for Mrs. Santigo. They were needed to help in the washing and cleaning up after the baby was born. You know what it is like when a colt is born. But in Jesus' day there were no pumps to use to get water. I think the innkeeper told Joseph to draw water from the well that all the village people used. Joseph would have had his own sheep-skin-leather bucket with him for they would need water on their journey to Bethlehem. What else have you been thinking about?"

"Well, I know that Jesus was wrapped in swaddling clothes and laid in the manger on the hay, but did Mary have sheets for the bed?"

This was a different thought. "People lived very differently then than we do now. Perhaps nobody used sheets in Jesus' day. But I am certain that Mary had woven all the clothes she would need for her little baby as well as what was needed for the journey."

"Did they take a trunk, Mama?"

"They were not rich people so they probably wore all the clothing they had and did not need a trunk."

"It's hard to think what it was like such a long time ago. I'm glad we have sheets on our beds," said Virgil as he wandered somberly off.

CHAPTER 62

Sledding

Yesterday Virgil was the happiest boy! For his Christmas gift Mac made the boy a sled. It is not only a sturdy piece of work, it has steel-clad runners on it. Most of the boys have to grease their wooden runners to get up a good speed. Virgil greases his runners, too, but at the end of the day, to prevent rust. We have had a good snow and Virgil says his steel-clad runners can go faster than any on the hill.

He is so proud of the gift and usually comes in from sledding glowing with satisfaction. This evening, however, he came in earlier to start on his chores and he did seem a bit more quiet than usual. I thought he had some serious schoolwork he was thinking about.

Mac came in from town just in time to sit down for supper. He and Virgil had no time to say more than, "Howdy." As soon as the blessing had been asked Mac was busy discussing his wagon load of orders that he would be bringing from California. What did we need or want, if anything? Virgil had nothing to say, which was unusual. All during supper he said only, "Pass the gravy, please."

At the end of the meal Mac leaned back in his chair and lighted his pipe. Virgil asked politely to be excused.

"Just a minute, young man," came Mac's serious response.

So, there was something on Virgil's mind and his Paw must know all about it.

"Yes, Sir," came the polite response, with Virgil's chin lower than usual.

"How was sledding today?"

"It was fine, Paw. Just fine. The snow is really hard packed." His enthusiasm increased. "And my steel runners slide so good." But Virgil's chin was lower even yet. Now what had the child been into?

"And how was the sledding on the southern end of Marina Street?" came Mac's incriminating question.

Marina Street, the choice street for all sledders, but prohibited to Virgil because it is too dangerous with its steep slope and blind curve. The sledder has no view of what wagon or carriages might be in the road as he suddenly comes whizzing around the turn and down that most perfect hill of all the sledding places. "Much too dangerous," Mac had pronounced.

"Well, uh, uh. It was good but I shouldn't have been there," came the slower response.

"What happened?" That stern question!

"Well, it happened like you said it would. There was a wagon right in my path and I couldn't stop and I couldn't get out of the rut I was in." The painful tale unfolded.

"Yes. Then what?"

"Well, Mr. Paulden pulled on the reins and stopped his team. I closed my eyes and went whizzing under the wagon."

"So, now what? Now that you are alive and didn't break up Mr. Paulden's wagon wheels or cause his team to run away?"

"Paw, I'm very sorry. I won't do it again. I apologized to Mr. Paulden, too."

"And do you know what else? You will have all winter to think about it. Grease those runners and put the sled away until next year. By then I think you will know which is the best hill for you to slide on."

Virgil mumbled a sorrowful, "Yes, sir." With quivering chin he went to get the beautiful sled.

I said nothing, but of course I thought the punishment was too harsh. All I could do was hope for no more snow.

CHAPTER 63

Earthquake: May 1887

Today I thought the hand of God had surely fallen on my shoulder. It was indeed a most strange occurrence.

I could not tell whether I was feeling giddy from the heat or what was happening. These unusually hot May days are more overbearing than any time I can remember. Since the death of my beloved Mother last month I am not always certain whether I am in a trance, about to swoon, or living outside my mind in another world.

I was certain the Lord was calling to me, calling attention to my ingratitude. Though we have lost our beloved one, the loving care and guiding hand of the Lord is forever with us. Even so, death, so cruelly final, is a difficult burden to bear. I keep my feelings to myself but perhaps I should not grieve so long over our loss. If the Lord in His infinite wisdom knows what is best for us frail mortals I must have been half expecting Him to tell me what to do.

I sat resting on the back stoop, still wearing my muddy garden clothes. With my head leaning against the door jamb I had fallen into a light slumber. Someone was shaking my shoulder, but I resisted wakening. I could not leave my rest.

There was no one near me. The shaking and booming had ceased. The sound that had wakened me was the hoe handle sliding across the house wall. The handle hit my bucket and fell to the ground. I sat thinking about the strange occurrence. I felt all right, even rested. I had heard no voice or voices. I was not so certain it was the Lord speaking to me.

Now footsteps sounded coming around the back door. I glanced down at my muddy shoes, smoothed my patched gardening apron and tucked some wisps of grey hair under my sunbonnet. Who could be coming?

Clearly the voice that called out to me was not Mac's. "Mother, did you feel the earthquake?"

"Earthquake?" I was completely taken aback. "Virgil?" I had supposed an earthquake would shake me right out of my shoes. Also, I now knew the hoe handle did not boom. And, I supposed the dear Lord would not necessarily lay his hand so gently on my shoulder.

I have not heard much about the earthquake that shook me awake yesterday. Mac explained that when you are right close to the earthquake you will know for sure what is happening. It will be much more than a hoe handle sliding across the wall.

I asked Mac to bring me a newspaper but they were all sold. Also the wires are down in the southern part of the Territory where the quake occurred and there is not yet very much known about what happened. I don't think the news will change much so it won't matter if I don't read about it until a few days later.

Mac suggested again that perhaps we should take the paper regularly. I still can't see much use in that. We get the news eventually from someone and we don't have to spend money for it.

Newspapers do have some uses after they have been read but I am not certain it is worth buying the paper just in case you could use it for something else after reading it. I had a friend in Ohio who liked to roll the paper in a tight roll, tie a string around it then tie it to a bar in her clothes press and there she had a nice hanger for a dress or shirt. Mac whittles hangers for me if I don't want to use a nail or a hook. I could have used a few papers to help start the cooking fire on that long journey back in 1865. Other than that I've not had a yen for the paper.

I don't have much time now to read all I'd like to read and I can't imagine having the chore of reading the paper every week. Men have more time to read than women do.

I must admit there is another thing I don't like about the newspaper. Some things in them are embarrassing. I glanced at a paper a few weeks back and there on the front page Mr. Goldwater had an advertisement about ladies corsets! No picture, mind you, but words an inch high. A shameless thing to have done! Right then I made up my mind what to do about newspapers!

At last we are getting the real story of the earthquake that knocked over my hoe handle. The hand of the Lord it was not. Such a mild tremor we had here. Even in Phoenix there was little cause to fret about it. However, some people, who were aware of it, would not leave their homes for several days.

For this reason some of the merchants put a note in a Phoenix newspaper to the effect there was no cause to interrupt commerce every time the wind blows or the earth trembles. It seems they were very upset that sales were a bit off for a couple of days. Laughable, indeed. Perhaps we should take up a collection for them!

The really severe part of the quake was not in Tombstone as we originally heard. It was farther south across the Mexican border in some little town I have never known of. Sadly, the people suffered. Some houses were demolished; there were some deaths and many injuries. We read that most of the people had very little of this world's goods to begin with. The cities in the southern part of the Territory are giving them some help.

Tombstone had some damage but not extensive. But damage is damage and it feels severe when it happens to you. Imagine having some good chinaware come crashing out of the cupboard onto the floor. Nothing left but bits and pieces. And it can never be replaced. A treasure gone is a severe loss.

There were a few houses in Tombstone that had been built on the side of a gully-arroyo, they call it. These houses were damaged so badly they could not be lived in safely. Not much more than shacks they were, but a home is a home and a person must have a place to lay the head.

Our Church group is getting together some household things to help the needy. We are caught a little short of things ourselves since we just finished sending off a missionary barrel to the church group in Oregon.

One of our church ladies asked the preacher something. I was a bit taken aback. At first it seemed an impertinent thing to question. The thing she put to him was why the good Lord would let such a terrible thing happen to His people.

Our kindly preacher was not a bit upset. He explained that there are things in nature that are going to happen. We know they will happen. Sometimes they will be destructive. If God stopped some things from happening and we were protected part of the time but not all of the time we would never be able to know what to depend on. Nature's laws are set and we must know we can depend on that, always.

CHAPTER 64

The Heating Stove

During this warm spell I decided it was a good time to take down the heating stove. A bit early, yes, for we will have a few more chilly days, but it will be good to be rid of the mess from wood carrying and cleaning out the ashes. Mac will miss his beautiful stove; it is a handsome thing and has heated our added room very well, but storing it in the woodshed will give more space here when I want to do some quilting. Besides, I need to get on with the spring cleaning before it is time to plant the garden.

It was well I rubbed my hands with tallow before we started taking down the stovepipe. The soot from the stovepipe was the worst I have ever seen. Mac says it is because we burned ponderosa pine most of the past winter. But pine we had so pine we burned, soot or no soot. Perhaps we can burn more oak next year when we won't have pine scraps from building the new room.

Now I am not certain it was such a good idea, but I especially planned this stove chore for Saturday to have Virgil's help, too. Certainly a ten year old can be depended on, I thought. He had the scrub bucket ready to set under the stovepipe the minute it was disjoined from the heater. Mac was very careful to handle the wobbly pipe so there was no soot spilling on the floor boards he is so proud of. The two of them carried the awkward load out. They watched their feet, they kept the pipe in the bucket and just as they stepped into the doorway the pipe hit the top of the door frame, and two pieces of piping fell back into the room, spilling soot everywhere. There was a slight breeze coming in that wafted the black stuff half way across the room.

I thought for certain Mac was going to let go an oath that would stop even the wind from stirring. He didn't. He nearly swallowed his chaw of tobacco, though. When he could speak he quietly directed Virgil to take the one upright pipe in the bucket out to the ash pile and be careful not to bend the pipe. Mac carefully lifted the remaining pipes, trailed Virgil to the ash pile, then stopped by the woodshed.

He brought back an old laprobe which he directed me to hold by a corner while we softly swept the dancing soot slowly out the door. He mixed it with the gravel and grit, shoveled it up into a barrel to haul far from home.

All this time he spoke not a word that was not necessary, I wasn't certain whether I'd laugh or cry so I kept quiet, too. Finally I did comment that I planned to keep back a tin can of soot to have in case of a bad cut that needed a mixture of soot and spider webs to staunch the blood flow. Can't be too careful to have things handy in a case like that. Mac nodded in agreement then suggested I get it out of the chimney before he covered the chimney hole.

The soot on the ash pile was carefully mixed into the ashes to keep them from blowing about. I didn't like that very much lest some black soot get into my soap-making ashes. But I reckoned I'd be careful. This did not seem just the right time to get fussy. We got the heavy stove out to the woodshed without incident though one time my tallow-slippery hands almost let go before we set the burden down safely.

I handed Virgil the blackening bottle to blacken the stove against rust. This was one time he could be put to this job without getting blackening on the carpet. He had a fine time and allowed no rust would we find on his blackened stove come frost time. His pride was shining through and right he was, too. There is little problem with rust in this dry place. The heater will look nice in the woodshed all summer and will need only a dusting before setting it up come cold weather.

Mac put up the cover over the chimney flue, I scrubbed the soot and tallow from my hands and I think Virgil's black spots will just have to wear off. That awful job is finished. Mac's beautiful floor has very few marks from the soot. As he said at supper time, they'll not be noticed on a galloping horse.

CHAPTER 65

Spring House Cleaning

It is a pleasure to sit for a bit of rest while I enjoy the greening of the trees. I have been so busy with this spring house cleaning I'd truly not noticed the leaves had sprung forth so vigorously since last week's rain. Mrs. Adams has a switch of a lilac bush she managed to bring all the way from Virginia. After services on Sunday last she told me it is beginning to put forth one head of blossoms. What a treasure.

In my spring cleaning I came across the peony corms I had brought from Mother's garden. If I were not so weary from lifting and cleaning I'd plant them now. Another day will do as well. I don't know where I can set them out that the cow won't crop them off. I think by the front door and I'll put a piece of wire fence about them so some wandering critter won't be causing me to fret.

My, how my back does ache from all that lifting. The rag rugs were the greatest burden. Even when I had the four strips ripped apart each one felt like a hundred pounds when I lifted it from the rinse water. I could have waited for Mac to return from town but he looks askance at all this disruption, as he calls it.

Well, a body can't abide having this dirt underfoot any longer; there's no way but to get down, move things about, rip the rugs apart and beat the sand and gravel out of them before putting them in the wash tub. That was when the heavy work began. I declare I think Mac decided rather suddenly that he needed to go to town. He didn't seem to need nails before he saw me ripping at the rugs. He could have been a great help at the beating. Or, as Mother used to say, "On the other hand (the one with the wart on it) men are not much help when they have made up their mind they don't want to help." She was so right. All in all, some things are easier to do alone.

Mac will bring me some clean straw from the livery stable when I'm ready to put the rugs down again. That will be a treat with the lofting of new straw under the rugs. I scarce can wait to hear the crinkling sound as the fresh straw is pressed underfoot. Virgil would like straw under his rug in the loft but of course too much would sift down from between the logs. Even if there was a sawed board floor there'd be the same mess.

Virgil is hoping for some special treat for all the extra water he is having to haul for the spring cleaning. I'll have to think of something. A taffy pull with Will would be fun.

CHAPTER 66

Sciatica

My, my, how Prescott has grown since our arrival in 1865. Ours is not the only log home here. Indeed, since the sawmill was built at Thumb Butte we have a sprinkling of sawed-lumber frame houses, too.

After spending our first winter in the borrowed log-and-tent house we have doubly appreciated the snug log house Mac built for us this past spring. Now I am so proud to be starting my first fall house cleaning in our dear little home.

I feel so satisfied to have my clean rug back on the floor. It was worth all the two weeks work. I lifted all the tacks myself for I wanted them to come out straight. Also, I alone ripped the rug strips apart. I wove those strips on the loom Mac made for me. I stitched them together and no one else shall lay scissors to them.

Virgil helped hang the strips on the line and by himself beat out the dirt. How the dust flew! While I ripped the next strip free, Virgil hauled the water from the creek to the two washtubs. He is a hard-working boy. Husband Mac carried off the old straw and grit from beneath the rug, and neat he was about it, too.

I did all the rub-a-dub scrubbing and the rinsing but Mac stayed nearby and helped me wring out the water. We all carried the wet burdens to the line to dry. Each was so heavy I thought the strong wire line would break. A 3'-by-12' piece of rug, wringing wet, is a great weight. The line held. It was the clothes pole that broke, letting the clean, wet rugs drag in the dirt. Then the rain came. It helped solve the dirt problem. Virgil was delighted to slop about in the wet weather and brush off the grit.

It was a good plan I had to take up only two strips at a time. Leaving the other two to be taken up later kept the room from looking so bare. With the steady drizzle of rain it will take a week for the two washed pieces on the line to dry. But of rain I will never be heard to complain. It is surely our most beloved gift from Heaven.

Another delay was my careless use of the rug needle. I was in a hurry sewing the last strip to the other three. Never does it pay to hurry a needle. I broke it and the next day had to walk over to Sam Hill Hardware to buy another. At the same time I was able to order from Ruffner's livery stable some clean straw to spread under my newly washed rug. No need to buy new tacks at this time, for the old ones came up very well. A penny saved is a penny earned.

I do like getting on my knees to nail the rug down. Mac has made a strong frame for the cushion I kneel on. It is easy to manage and the task goes faster. The hammering I truly enjoy. Mac says it's how I get all the anger out of my bones.

I declare I think I hammered too much yesterday for there is the most dreadful ache in my hip and on down my right limb. I feel so good about having my rug clean, stitched and tacked back on the floor, yet now I can scarcely bend over at the fireplace to cook.

I do not know what has come over me to have this pain. Mac says for certain I am having a bout with sciatica. His Mother had the ailment and suffered terrible pain. He remembers what she did to get relief. No use studying the doctor book. Mac says I won't learn what to do and the doctor won't do me any good either.

Well, mercy on us, I certainly would not have the doctor come by to tell me what to do for just a pain in my limb.

Mac says if I will stand in the doorway to brace myself, he will give my leg a good pull and the pain will be gone and over with. I think I will have him try it tonight if I am still hurting. It's a terrible thing to limp about. Best that I wait until Virgil is asleep though. It wouldn't be seemly for him to see his father holding me by my limb.

This morning all is well. My Dr. Mac knows how to cure a body, for my pain is entirely gone. My newly washed rug is a delight to behold. In addition there is the delicate scent and the crunch, crunching of the clean straw underfoot.

CHAPTER 67

Our Second Wage Earner

Since Mac is indisposed with the ague he has not been taking any orders for delivery of goods from California. That means of course we have had but little cash coming in. I manage to get a pittance from the butter and egg money and can make do with the few things I must buy. I have said nothing about the situation but Virgil was aware that cash was low. Today he came in all aglow. He has a job after school working in the print shop.

After the news of his employment he asked, as though petitioning me,"Mama, you don't mind if they call me a printer's devil, do you?" I smiled as I shook my head.

I declare, I was so taken aback I hardly knew what to say. Of course I was mighty proud that he had the git up and git to do this all on his own at twelve years of age. I asked him if he intends to put his money in the bank. He allowed he'd just give it to me for right now. If his wages go up five cents more a day he said he might split it with me. Very generous, I thought.

Virgil was very keen on explaining how the type setters set the type for printing. He doesn't do that kind of work yet. There is a composing stick which is not a stick at all but a tray just the right height for the letters. Each letter is placed on the composing stick upside down and the words are backwards, mind you. The words or sentences are held in place by the frame of the stick and wooden wedges make the letters fit tightly. The stick is then set into the chase and locked in for printing. I understood him but it would be necessary to see it to believe it.

Virgil says the printing press machine is almost as big as his bed and weighs a ton at least. It has to be so big and heavy both to keep the machine steady and to press the inked letters onto the paper. I declare I do not see how Secretary McCormick could bring that heavy thing with him all the way from Missouri and across the rough country that we crossed. We had trouble enough carrying our food and water. It truly shows the importance of the printed word.

Virgil was telling me how hard it was to pick out the right size letters every time. I think putting everything upside down and backwards would be the hard part. I always knew Virgil to be a smart boy but if he has to think words upside down and backwards I think he'll soon be holding his reading the same way. Landsakes! What will become of his learning!?

And being called a Printer's Devil. Such a name! But of course I don't mind. Mac and I both are so very proud of him.

CHAPTER 68

Printers' Pranks

Things are a bit better about the place. Mac is feeling stronger. I'm devising things for him to do. Whittling he enjoys most. He has finished a hammer handle for himself. Now he's reshaping the edge of the dust pan for me. It keeps him indoors and out of the cold.

Such a cough he has. I've put onion poltices on his chest for a night though I can't see that it's quieted him much. Even the cough medicine I keep giving him has plenty of onion juice in it. I guess the cough will just have to run its course. But he must stay in and keep warm.

I was carrying a tray of hot tea to Mac when Virgil sailed through the house. He had finished his after-school work as a printer's devil. He ran up the ladder to the loft to change to his play clothes. I did not really get a good look at the child. He called down from above that he was going sledding but would be back before dark to split kindling for the morning fire.

My thought was he would not get much sledding in before dark, though these February days are lengthening. He would have a few minutes of fun. He was soon scooting down the ladder and out the door, throwing a red scarf about his neck as he made his escape.

My, such energy, I thought, and went to the range to shake the grate and bring the fire up for baking cornbread. The bean soup has simmered all day. It's Virgil's and Mac's favorite supper.

In a short time I heard the ax. Virgil was true to his word. Dark was descending and soon I'd need to light the coal-oil lamp. Virgil came in with a good arm load of neatly split pieces. He had enough to last for three days. As he passed me to get to the wood box behind the range, I had a glimpse of Virgil's face that made me think "Measles?"

Hurriedly I lighted the lamp to get a better look before the child got out of my sight again. His hand was on the doorknob as he sang out, "I'll bring in a load of wood, Mama."

I waited patiently with the lamp, determined to get a good look this trip around. In he came, stomping his feet well in the door step. "Put the wood in the box," I said. "Then I want to get a good look at you."

He wore a silly grin as I remonstrated, "What in heaven's name is on your face?"

"Oh, Mama, its just printer's ink. I tried to get it off but some stayed on I guess."

"But how did you…..? His face was speckled as a black Plymouth Rock hen.

"The men at the print shop were just funnin' and they squeezed the type in some way that made it pop up just as they told me to look down real close for some printer's lice. They knew there weren't any lice, but I didn't know for sure. Everything came flying out and spattered me. But it was only fun, except 'twasn't very much fun picking up all those tiny little letters off the floor and getting them back ready for printing. I wished they were paying me by the hour and not by the week. But we didn't have very much type to be set today."

"Come, I'll get some Vaseline. That will probably clean you up, along with some soap and hot water. Lampblack and coal oil is not so easy to get off."

I set the lamp down and thought to myself, grown men acting like silly little boys. I said nothing for I knew if Mac's opinion was asked he'd have sided with the men for having a little fun. Well, anyway, we do get the newspaper free each week.

CHAPTER 69

Night of Fire, July 14, 1900

At one time or another one or more amongst us has suffered sorely. Always we have rallied and aided each other in such times. No one here has had to bear a burden alone.

Now a great calamity has fallen on our whole city. One entire section of our city center has burned to the ground. A lifetime of effort, 40 years, is gone in one night. Now I know how much I have grown to love this town. The disaster seems more than any of us can bear.

Last night a gathering of terrified women stood at Marina Street crossing looking down into the horror below. Some were forcibly restrained from going farther on Gurley Street. Their husbands and sons were down there fighting the fierce flames while a demonic wind fanned the conflagration. It was not one or two buildings flaring. The whole of Montezuma Street's Whiskey Row was burning. Our men could not stem the tide of flowing fire.

Worse yet, a long drought in this hot summer has drained our insufficient water supply. The four wells, dug long ago at the four corners of the Courthouse Plaza, have not been used for the past ten years. They were uncovered and found empty and useless in the emergency. It was heartbreaking to see the flames jump the street and race up Gurley Street. Firebrands shot high into the air, torching adjoining buildings.

We heard cries of warning as charred roofs fell in, scattering the glowing flames. Firemen shouted directions above the explosion of whiskey barrels. Pleas for help drifted thinly here and there. Screams of pain, the frightened whinnying of horses were dimmed in the roar and crackle of the fire.

The air, filled with burning horsehair, was blown full to our faces. The acrid smell of fiery destruction was more than we could endure. Some women felt too ill to stay and were taken away by kindly neighbors.

Everywhere heat and smoke roiled furiously. The mindless demon, fire, gathered the town center in an embrace of charred ruin. The weary heroic men finally prevented the burning from spreading. They dynamited a few standing buildings to smother and quench the determined fire.

Dawn's faint rays lighted five city blocks of black, crumbled, brick walls. They stood broken, mutely naked among curls of smoke and broken metal.

At sunup the American flag was raised. The bugler sounded the call to duty. Prescott will go on. With spirit our city will live, grow, and thrive.

CHAPTER 70

The Auto Complaint, 1909

Surely I should think of something worthwhile to do today but these automobile problems have been fretting me for some time now. I am of a mind to think them through.

Perhaps we should have outlawed such a machine when they first appeared on the streets. But, of course, the men like them. An auto is a grown man's toy. That's all they are. Women folk know them for the noisy and smelly things we can do without.

I am surprised this gasoline wonder does not explode as it goes pop, pop, popping down the street. It is clear very few owners know how to care for them. Sometimes it seems five or six men will work over a faulting auto for hours before they find out what is wrong and get the thing started again. And the way horses are frightened of the roaring motor is reason enough to have outlawed such a dangerous contrivance. Now it is too late. It will never come to pass. Men have clasped the auto to their bosom as though it were a woman.

Certainly the auto has different hazardous characteristics to consider. In the newspaper the other day was the report of a man who was cranking up his motorcar. Somehow the crank popped loose with great force, hit the man's arm and broke it. He had to have the doctor come to set his arm and put it in a cast. There was another story of a man making a sharp turn too fast. The machine wheeled over, the man fell out under the auto. There was no door to keep him in. He was killed. A dreadful situation and final. It didn't hurt the machine much. I understand the widow got rid of the thing next day.

Speed seems to be the thing that causes most of the problems. I can't understand why velocity is so important to the men. In the "Tucson Daily and Weekly Citizen" I read the police have trouble keeping the automobile drivers from racing about town. The limit is set at seven miles an hour. That should be enough to satisfy a body. Yet the men encourage more speed all the time by staging automobile races. No sense to it. I wonder how the police apprehend the speeders. On horseback, I presume.

I suppose it is important to get somewhere more quickly if a body has a long trip. When we traveled from Ohio to Prescott by oxen and covered wagon, 44 years ago, I surely would have enjoyed going a bit faster. Last Fall "The Arizona Republic" staged the first Arizona auto race. Four men joined the competition. What a stir that made. It took a lot of planning for enough water, gas, oil and equipment. I don't remember what happened to three of them, but the winner, in spite of tribulations, drove from Los Angeles to Phoenix in less than two days. A little bit more than 41 hours as I recollect. That was surely a remarkable thing to do. It takes Mac two weeks, at least, to make that trip and he has some fast moving mules. The winner allowed it would have been a shorter trip for him but he mired in the sand and had several flat tires. He let on he intends to try again and take less time. Without a doubt someone will figure a way to speed things up. Well, just let it be out on the open road.

It does seem to me they could drive a respectable, steady pace about town and show more consideration for people who are afoot. We women can scarce cross the street sometimes. When it is muddy I stay home. Those big tires are larger around than my wrist and can splash mud up onto the boardwalk. Speeding makes it worse. Seven miles an hour is fast enough, but mark my word, it will be no time until the rate is set at ten. Right there is where they should peg it, for good and forever, I say.

CHAPTER 71

Runaway Car

Mac came home yesterday with the funniest tale about old Mr. J.J. Allen. Mac's first unkind words I almost agree with: "Old J.J. has more money than brains." I am disposed to believe it is only these later years that have found his mind confused.

It seems Old J.J. had driven his auto from the carriage house without his son knowing about it. J.J. Jr. keeps a tight rein on his elderly father who, in his dotage, is like a spoiled child and does pretty much as he pleases if not apprehended.

Of course with a self starter there was no need to crank up the vehicle. The poor old man would have been better off if he'd had more trouble starting. He drove the dazzling Reo out onto Alarcon and turned west onto Gurley. From there on Mac said it was pure bedlam.

"I can't stop it!," the old fellow began screaming. "Whoa, whoa! Help!" His cries of panic were heard in every house on the street, and doors flew open in a jiffy. Neighbors are accustomed to his voice and his antics.

"Help! I can't stop it! Whoa! Ho back!," he shouted his commands. He tugged at the steering wheel as though he held the reins of a team of horses.

Squawking chickens flapped across in front of him, dogs came barking and snapping at the speeding wheels. Women screamed and children ran from his direction or positioned themselves safely behind a tree, still wanting a ringside view.

The helpless driver passed the Marina Street crossing. The speed increased on the downward pitch toward Courthouse Square. Few, if any, knew how to stop the contraption. The whole town, shopkeepers and customers, stopped to stare. No one dared clamber aboard the racing vehicle to rescue the poor old man. Some men ran to the hitching rail and grabbed the bits of their frightened horses. Two teams approaching Gurley from Cortez reared up in their traces. The frightened whinnying blended in with the uproar. The halted teams stopped two other autos whose drivers blasted out with their horns and cussed at the teamsters until they saw the predicament with the speeding runaway.

The well-rutted road kept the auto in a fairly straight path. His cries of "whoa" fell faintly as he coasted up West Gurley then rolled back to a stop at Granite Creek. The Sheriff stepped out from a nearby bar and appraised the scene just as the vehicle halted. The driver, astonished at stopping, now tried frantically to open his auto door. The lawman gave assistance and the frightened Mr. Allen, with beet-red face, stepped out.

"Infernal machine," spat the furious old fellow.

"Young Sprout," Sheriff remarked quietly, "I'm going to have to take you in for speeding and disturbing the peace."

Nothing of the sort happened, of course. Young J.J. came shaking his head in disbelief. "Paw," he asked gently, "what have I told you about driving this automobile? Come on, get in. I'll take you for a ride."

Off they roared and Old J.J., now smiling, waved to the crowd, not at all abashed for the furor he had caused.

CHAPTER 72

The Forgotten Fried-Egg Quilt?

Virgil, now 49 years of age, is a fine man. It surely is a blessing to have him travel with his father on the trips to fill the miners' orders. I'm not certain Mac would be able to do the work alone though he is in good health. Thankfully we all three are so blessed. I'm certain the outdoor life we all enjoyed is the reason for our good health.

The man whom Mac and Virgil have brought in tonight for me to "doctor up" is not one I can do much for. I'll call the doctor in tomorrow. Thank goodness for telephones.

Virgil happened to see the poor fellow lying beside the road as he and Mac came home this afternoon. He was resting and needed the ride into Prescott to find work in the mines, he said. He has a bad cough and I'm certain he needs care and nourishment.

It may be a tad farfetched, but Virgil seems to think the tattered blanket the poor fellow had over his shoulders looks like his old fried-egg quilt. And what's more, he thinks when the fellow is better able to talk, we may learn he is Joseph the Miracle Boy. Long ago we found the lad lost on the Santa Fe Trail, and took him back to Sante Fe in our wagon.

As a little child he had been snatched away by Indians. They gave him to a grieving Indian mother whose infant had died. Joseph was called Small Boy by his Indian family. He was happy but always remembered the words "Santa Fe."

We learned at the Santa Fe Inn how to find the parents. There was great rejoicing over Joseph the Miracle Boy. It was then that Virgil had presented his precious fried-egg quilt to Joseph to remember their Sante Fe friendship.

Now, Virgil feels certain the fried-egg quilt has brought the two friends, now grown, together again.

0-595-32745-1

1844681